Work Stories
by
Marty Nemko

6th printing, revised and expanded

Copyright © Marty Nemko 2024

Marty Nemko

Praise for Marty Nemko

"Magnificent food for thought." Walter Block, Wirth Eminent Scholar, Loyola U.

"Delectable bite-sized, short stories...It's difficult to stop reading them." Dr. Mark Goulston, author of *Just Listen*.

"Some unusual subjects to say the least! I highly recommend this worthwhile read." Michael Edelstein, author of *Three-Minute Therapy*.

"One of the few truly original thinkers of our time." Kathryn Riggs, retired, U.C. Berkeley School of Education."

"A really smart person." Michael Scriven, former president, American Evaluation Association.

"The best of the best." Warren Farrell, author, *The Myth of Male Power*.

Marty Nemko

- Award-winning career and personal coach.

- Author of 32 books, from *Careers for Dummies* to *Light: short-short stories on life's brighter side*.

the author, own work

- Ph.D., educational psychology, University of California Berkeley.

- Enjoys giving talks and being interviewed, playing concerts of show tunes and standards on the piano, acting in plays, hybridizing roses, and his sweet doggie, Hachi.

- Marty's first job was, at age 13, barroom piano player. At 20, he drove a taxicab in New York City.

To people who work beyond the minimum.

Dear Reader,

I welcome your honest review of this book on Amazon as well as your email. I promise to respond. My email address is mnemko@comcast.net

Marty Nemko

Marty Nemko

Work Stories

Contents

Black Then Red 11
Quit? 12
Remote 14
The Emperor's New Clothes (DEI version) 17
What a Hotel Bar Pianist is Thinking 18
Ripples 19
A Whistleblower's Tale 20
A Dose of Reality 22
A World Without Men 25
A Telemarketer with a Soul 29
One Way to Get a Promotion 31
Kamal 32
Jokester Janitor 34
The World's Kindest IRS Agent 35
Chill Coaching 38
Fantasy Traffic School 40
Kansas to Vegas 43
Sam's Last Concert 46
A Therapist Support Group 49
Trying 51
A Perfectionist Conductor 52
Faith Shaken 54
Reduction 55
Double Promotion 57
The Hope Giver 58
"It's Not My Job to Make You Coffee" 60
Thoughts in Class 62
Robin Hood, The Meter Man 63
Sowing Oats 65
Unseen 66
Recipes from the IRS 68
The Carpenter 70
The Warehouse Pairer 72
Advanced Objections Training 73
A Cheese Clerk Talks to His Dog 76

A Magical Teacher 77
They Tried to Get Rid of Me 79
The Laziest Person 80
Power Imbalance 81
In Tune 82
A Cop in Bed 84
Norma 86
The Toilet Cleaners' Union 88
Big Balls 89
Burn 94
Do What You Love? 96
A MD and His Starving-Artist Child 98
53 and Unhirable 100
No Fuckin' Way 102
I Can't Even Give Away My Books 103
Grandpa's Beg 105
The Barkery and Me 107
A Salesman Turned Fundraiser Talks to His Dog 108
A Dancer Talks to Her Dog 109
A Musician Talks to His Dog 110
Warrior and "Wimp" 111
Puff Piece 112
Astronaut or Homemaker? 114
A Coffee Tree Grows in Brooklyn 116
A Seven-Fingered Pianist 119
BeautEase Roses 120
Just When You Feel Safest 122
"Workers of the World, Unite!" 123
Feedback 125
A Lazy Career Coach 126
A Burned-Out Teacher 141
Merit 143
All-Star 145
A Dropout 146
A Cheery Chemo Nurse 148
A Psychiatrist's Last Hour 150
Boring Man 154

Work Stories

A Lonely College President 156
Redistributor.. 157
While I Can.. 158
The 50-Year Secretary, Oops, Admin 160
"Should I Follow My Dad or Mom?".. 162
A School Bus Driver... 163
The Biggest Molecule... 164

Marty Nemko

Work Stories

Black Then Red

Reggie wanted a promotion. No, he needed a promotion. He was burned out on being a beat cop and even though police pay was high in the Bay Area, rent was higher still.

With permission, 18/1 Graphics Studio

Reggie's mentor advised, "There always are openings in the bomb squad. And mainly you just sit around— There aren't that many bombs to dismantle. Take the course."

Reggie did and was taught that bomb dismantling is less complicated than it might seem. Mainly, you just have to first cut the black wire that connects to the detonator and, only then, the red wire.

Reggie applied for the next opening in the bomb squad and, to his surprise, was hired over people with experience.

"Maybe I did really well in the interview."

Indeed, in Reggie's two months on the job, there were no bombs to dismantle. The squad just did simulations— Find the detonator, cut the black wire, then the red one. Easy-peasy.

Then, off-duty on a Saturday night, Reggie took his kids to a concert. A row ahead, from a backpack underneath a seat, he heard ticking.

Reggie used his foot to slide the backpack toward him. The ticking was louder. He pulled the backpack's zipper to see inside. It was a bomb and it was easy to find its detonator.

Then he saw that the two wires were purple and orange.

Quit?

Courtesy, WestEnd61

I'm 40 and am still best friends with Derek, the kid who sat next to me in the 3rd grade.

Although we both live in LA, because of the traffic, we just talk on the phone or Zoom. But today for once, we decided to brave the traffic to meet for coffee.

Before we go further, I should explain that Derek and I are testimony to opposites attracting. I value stability. For example, I'm one of the administrative assistants at one of L.A's. county's many regulatory boards and commissions. https://tinyurl.com/29p8jzz8 I'm embarrassed at how bureaucratic it is: Even on minor matters, we have rules and regulations often requiring a petitioner to provide detailed information and then we often deny the request or ask for more data. But the job pays well and we get good benefits and great job security. On the personal front, I'm married, we just had our second child, and I try to be a responsible husband and father. We own a modest condo in one of L.A

County's only decent school districts. For fun, I like watching high school sports and TV shows like Ted Lasso and Shark Tank.

Derek is the opposite. He's an entrepreneur. The product doesn't matter as long as it sells. One time it was recycled wind-turbine parts. Then it was a new flavoring for Listerine-knockoff mouthwash, and then there was a lower-cost tool-and-die-making machine. Lest you think Derek is a zillionaire, he always complains of "cash flow" problems, which he only partly keeps at bay by delaying paying bills and getting credit cards that are 0% interest for the first year. On the personal front, he's a fun-loving bachelor and vacations in cool places, from Cannes to Cancun.

Not surprising, Derek showed up in a Nike track suit and Hoka shoes while I wore my usual no-brand polo, jeans, and sneakers.

Even though Derek and I know each other well, we started with small talk like, "Boy, the Lakers suck again." I transitioned by asking, "So, Derek, how's business?" He said, "I found a formula for longer-lasting chewing gum." But when I asked whether he's had it medical tested, he said, "Uh, we're not up to that yet. Uh, Matt, how's your job?"

I said, "Steady-Eddie: The paychecks keep coming, the job is chill, and the government matches my 401k. It's okay."

He snorted, "Dude, you're 40, half done. Is that really all you want: chicken-shit, fear-driven make-work government bureaucrat? It's the embodiment of soul-sucking."

All I could muster was, "It isn't so bad and it's great to know the paychecks will always come in — unlike your career, Derek."

He replied, "You just had a kid. So take advantage of the Family and Medical Leave Act. The feds give you 12 weeks off, the state adds another 12, and voila, you've got almost a half year to come up with something better.

I said I'd think about it but between you and me, I don't think I have the guts.

Remote

I had just gotten out of bed and so had to use my palm-tree background for the Zoom. Of course, that fools no one — There are no palm trees in Indiana.

CoolArts223, Deviant Art, CC 3.0

They had finished the two-minutes of grace and small talk, whereupon the boss revealed what he calls, My Big Idea of the Fiscal Quarter: "We're going to replace our capri-pants line with wide-bottoms — It's blowing up in L.A.!"

Everyone nodded enthusiastically except me. I couldn't believe people really like that idea — It was a retread of what was hot and then not 30 years ago, then 15 years ago, and here we are again. But even though all bosses say they welcome disagreement; most don't. It's safest to agree.

"Great to see all the agreement," he gushed. He ignored my flat face and just rolled on: "So, on to materials. How about recycled plastic made to look like leather?" Again, unanimous nods. Even I nodded, although with less fervor.

Onto the logo. One person said, "How about a weed plant?" The boss said, "Legal would stop it. How about —looking at my palm-tree background — How about a palm with one leaf that looks a *little* like a weed leaf?" More nods.

"Great. We're making huge progress. On to color palette. My thought is to go bold. Instead of Protest Black and Soviet Gray like everyone else, let's go colored. I said, only half joking, "Watch that phrasing."

"Ok, let's go *of*-color. Ideas on palette?" Everyone enjoys talking color — It requires no intelligence and everyone has an opinion. Blue and pink were immediately rejected because of "sexism potential." Then a flurry of proposals and rejections of oranges and yellows. They ended up leaning toward purple, tan, and green.

The boss said, "We gotta give them market-edgy names. There was more flurry followed by consensus on Astral Aubergine, Tawdry Taupe, Coconut Cricket (light green) and my contribution, obviously for giggles only: pukey puce.

But the boss took me seriously. "Pukey Puce: — It's so bad, it's good. We'll get tons of word-of-mouth, especially among our target market: stupid teens, useful idiots. One person chimed, "Yeah, our logo could be a pukey puce palm!" Everyone laughed, even me.

I tried another joke: "How about a two-tone: red and green, not for Christmas, but a watermelon pattern." They nodded but without comment, which I assumed was the Midwestern way of saying, "No way, Jose."

The boss said, "Now to advertising. Key today is biracial, non-binary. Blacks are expensive these days but maybe we could land a Black and an Asian gender-ambiguous couple to be our poster kids."

Someone asked in a fake Hispanic accent, "But won't that offend the Latin*X*?" I added, "We could make it a threesome. Polyamory is in." Only one person thought I was serious. But someone seriously asked, "What about a white man?" The boss said, "Maybe they'll be 'in' next year." I thought, "I doubt it."

Just then, I got a text from a woman who was responding to my match.com ad. I had to look. "I was intrigued by your profile and am wondering…" I was awakened by the boss, "Don, you've been quiet. How should we configure the focus groups?"

I said, "For once, I'll be honest — I don't know and I don't care. Adios." Of course, I was fired.

Well today, I was leafing through a trade mag and saw my former company's full-page color ad picturing superwide pants made of recycled plastic — in Christmas Watermelon. (See above.)

The Emperor's New Clothes (DEI version)

I'm the head of the DEI caucus at the Silicon Valley Institute of Technology.

They call me "loud 'n 'proud" and they should. I *am* loud n' proud. Like at my last call-to-arms meeting, I preached,

PNGFree, CC

BIPOCs are ever more the victim of systemic racism, oppression by the white male patriarchy. Their demanding excellence, virtuosity, even merit is just a white supremacist value and an excuse to avoid DEI: diversity, equity, and inclusion. We must be as one, we-not-me, all in. But not just equality but equity, a term we redefined from fairness to giving us our deserved advantage after 150 years of the legacy of slavery — reparations! People of the World, especially intersectionalists, UNITE!"

Although I didn't get a standing ovation, everyone cheered, even chanted, — UNITE, UNITE, UNITE. A few white and Asian males didn't cheer. I think they were afraid to disagree and show what racists they are. And then, the oldest white male in the room — He was 50 if he was a day — stood up.

He said,

Replacing merit with melanin reduces all of us to a lower common denominator, hurting everything from our coworkers to our college, from customer care to medical care. You should be ashamed of yourself.

Everyone stared at me, then at each other. Next, one person applauded *him* and slowly, every white and Asian male and even some women(!) stood up. They gave *him* a standing ovation. They're a bunch of fuckin' racists!

What a Hotel Bar Pianist is Thinking

After 30 years playing piano at the same hotel bar, you're kind of on autopilot, so your mind is free to wander. I thought you might enjoy knowing some of my mind's musings:

The author, Photo credit: Dianne Woods

No one really cares about whether I play wonderfully or not. Most people are there to veg, flirt, think, or network, and so on. The piano player? It could as easily be Muzak. Still, I try to play as though I was at Carnegie Hall.

It's fun to see people's get-ups. They're usually for effect, for example, to impress, flirt, or be a hipster. I'm guessing that the ones who come to my fancy hotel in grungies are trying to give the finger to capitalism or to traditional beauty.

If you watch people, you usually can see who's on the make, who wants to be left alone, couples in love or who are bored with each other.

Work Stories

The guy gave his motormouth companion all sorts of signals that he was bored and overwhelmed: He sighed, tried to interrupt her, even turned away, but that Energizer Bunny kept going and going, rapid-fire like a pitchman trying to cram a too-long script into a 30-second commercial. God, so many of us, even those who claim to care about The Other, can be so self-absorbed.

Then there are the occasionally women I mentally undress — harmless fun.

All right, I should be good. I think I'll play Over the Rainbow.

Ripples

I was being practical. I would have rather majored in music but I sucked it up and did business.

YourFavLoaf, DeviantArt, CC

After I graduated, I sent out 146 applications — I counted — for like, management trainee positions and all I got were three screening interviews, a dozen rejections, and mostly silence.

My dad kept asking me to come work at his factory. But he's just a foreman in a plant that makes machines that seal plastic bags, you know, like Doritos bags.

I kept saying no. If the only job I can get is through my father, I'm a loser — How could I tell my friends, let alone a girl. Plus, the job would be dull, low pay, dead-end. I worked hard for five, count 'em five — years at college and it cost my parents $200,000 — and that was a state school. I still have $116,000 in student loans and they can't be discharged in bankruptcy. And now I was going to take a job I could have gotten as a high school dropout? But with that huge loan hanging over me, I took it.

It was clanging; it was dirty; it was repetitive. Yeah, it felt good getting good at the job and I now respect people who do grungy work, but still. I'm thinking of quitting and getting an MBA.

But even if I could get in somewhere, I'm not that smart and I am kind of a procrastinator, so I'm not sure if more years in school would be a better use of my time than staying in bag-sealing. Plus, I'm scared that even if I took on another $100,000 in student debt, I still wouldn't get past the screening interviews.

But is that all there is to life: a hobby of playing guitar at open-mic nights and a career of making sure Doritos-bag seams' ripples are tight?

A Whistleblower's Tale

I graduated from social work school eager to apply what I was taught: Fight to redistribute more taxpayer resources to the poor.

The federal govt buildings where I live, Oakland, CA. Photo credit: Library of Congress

Work Stories

So I was thrilled to get a job at the U.S. Department of Urban Programs...until I got up to my workgroup's office. It was 8:30, the required starting time, yet most of the desks were empty and the few people there were reading a newspaper, one was even polishing her nails.

I soon learned that while the required workday is 8:30 to 4:30, most employees came in late and left early. The boss didn't seem to care. Indeed, he too usually arrived around 9:30 and left at 2:30. When I asked him about it, he smiled, "We're family-friendly here. Many of us have to get our kids to school and pick them up."

I was tempted to object but was too scared to — As a new employee, I was on probation and didn't want to lose that potentially contributory and, okay, cushy job — Even if I worked the full eight-hour day, that was less than my husband works, and we get every holiday and ample personal days, full health care, even a pension, plus great job security — To lose your job, you practically have to call someone a racial epithet.

But I was having trouble sleeping, thinking of all the poor people who were being deprived because of my lazy coworkers. But I knew that whistleblowing is rarely successful and despite the whistleblower laws, many whistleblowers end up leaving their job. But I couldn't live with myself so I wrote to the Office of the Inspector General.

A few weeks later, something happened, but not what I had hoped. I received a letter from the IRS telling me that I was selected for a full audit. Me, who earns just a moderate W-2 income? I guessed that my boss used the IRS to punish me for blowing the whistle. I confronted him and he admitted it but shrugged.

I went to the media, all of which ignored me, except one news organization that I hate so much I won't even mention its name, like the way I call Trump "45." That news organization's website ran just a short piece but I got a call from a lawyer me asking if I wanted to sue.

She got me a $400,000 settlement, a guarantee I would not lose my job, and mysteriously, the audit was called off. The IRS wrote, "Our error. You are not to undergo the audit."

A Dose of Reality

This story is essentially true. Only irrelevant details have been changed.

F_a_r_e_w_e_l_l, Flickr. CC 2.0

Tom got a doctorate in education and everyone was sure he'd become a professor preparing graduate students for a career as a K-12 teacher.

But in Tom's fieldwork, it was clear to him that he was far from a master teacher. He couldn't even control difficult students. Tom had learned a lot of theory but too little that was practical.

So after completing his doctorate, he decided he needed to get practical experience to see if he could become a good teacher. So, he took a job in one of Boston's high schools that are sanitizingly called "challenged."

It soon became clear to Tom that many of the students, especially the active boys, had a hard time sitting through a 50-minute period and especially the double periods that education experts advocate.

So Tom decided that during a double period, he'd take his class on a little field trip. The problem was that half of the students didn't return the parent permission slip. It wasn't that the parents weren't willing to sign. The slips too often didn't get to the parents. Tom's students said they lost it, their parents were away, and so on. He gave them another permission slip but still, many didn't come back.

So Tom decided to try a trip with all the kids, even if some didn't have a permission slip. He thought, "It's just to the nearby tide pool." He rented a 15-person van and packed his class into it. (If a bit scrunched, they'd all fit in the van because while his class size was officially 22, on an average day, only 15 would show.)

Everyone had a great time. And to ensure that they were addressing the mandated Common Core Curriculum, they discussed and Tom gave assignments that tied the trip to academic learning.

So, a week later, they did another trip. This time, it was a behind-the-scenes tour of a bakery. Another success.

Unfortunately, the third time, when the kids were getting into the van, this time to go to a museum, the principal saw them aghast—"Mr. Johnson, don't you know that our insurance doesn't cover that!? And did you get permission slips from all the parents?"

Tom murmured no, she pulled him aside, and said, "I am initiating termination procedures. You are endangering your students."

Of course, Tom was sad, scared, but also angry—He wanted to prioritize his students and as a result, he was getting fired?! So that very Friday, he asked his class, "Who'd like to spend the weekend in my apartment with my family?" Nearly everyone raised their hand. There wasn't enough room in Tom's apartment for all the students but his classroom aide volunteered to let some stay with her. The next morning, Tom asked his aide, "So how'd it go?" She said, "Two of them raped me."

Tom lamented not just the loss of his job but that he had tried so hard to be a good teacher, and his aide was so kind, so patient. How could two of their students do that? How dare they? Tom thought, "I'm not sure what to believe anymore."

The teachers union defended Tom but he lost his job anyway. He thought about taking some innocuous job like clerk in a bookstore but accepted a position at a university—training prospective teachers.

A World Without Men

Thought experiments are no-risk ways to explore extreme ideas in hopes that "thinking outside the box" will spawn new realistic ideas. Besides, I find it fun to contemplate thought experiments. Perhaps you will too.

Jim Linwood, Flickr, CC 2.0

I've written a number of thought experiments. Today's: What positives and negatives would accrue from a world without men? For fun, I've lent this an air of parody.

The year is 2050. Society's view of the male gender has changed. The 1950s venerated men. In the early through mid-2000s, the male gender was perceived as, on average, inferior. That was encapsulated in many private conversations among women in which it was agreed that "Men suck." And now in 2050, the President of the United States, Jezebel Jones, issued an Executive Order to eliminate all men.

So she ordered Compound Z, a pathogen that causes men to instantly die but is harmless to women, to be released from all surveillance cameras in the U.S, which surreptitiously double as drug dispensers, whether to enhance health such as aerosol vaccines or to, well, kill. To ensure the extermination was fully executed, she also ordered the Army, Navy, Air Force, and Marines to release Compound Z throughout even lightly populated areas, from airplanes, helicopters, and tank turrets. She ordered the National Guard and welfare recipients to remove the dead carcasses.

At the press conference, a reporter asked, "But what about the men who survive?" President Jones said, "They'd have to remain in their shelter forever, whereupon, like flies stuck on fly paper, they'll soon die."

What might occur?

Of course, in the real world, generalizations about a gender are dangerous and are often over-generalizations. But in the real world, we do often make policy that applies only to a specific demographic, for example, reparations, scholarships for a particular demographic, and different standards for college admission, hiring, and awarding contracts. With that caveat, here are my hypotheses as what might accrue from a world without men.

Fewer wars, although it wouldn't eliminate war. A small fraction of wars have been started by women. Cleopatra launched a war against Egypt. Britain's Queen Anne started one in North America that was named after her. In 1971, India's Prime Minister, Indira Gandhi started a war against Pakistan. In 1973, after a surprise attack on Israel by Arabs on the Jewish people's holiest day (Yom Kippur), prime minister Golda Meir launched and won a brief war against Egypt. UK Prime Minister Margaret Thatcher started a war against the Falkland Islands — not a fair fight.

Less violent crime. While women may perpetrate other sorts of malfeasance, the large majority of violent crime is committed by men. No men, less violent crime.

Less competition, more collaboration. Of course, some women lean toward competition and men toward collaboration but, on average, women tend to be more collaborative.

More collaboration yields the advantages of more input and buy-in in decision-making, and some projects are best when tasks are divvied up.

On the other hand, collaboration tends to decrease individuals' ownership. Also, group decision-making can result in tepid solutions, that lowest common denominator that the group can agree on. Plus, some tasks are better done by an individual — more investment, fewer communication snafus, and less frustration about team members who don't pull their weight.

More work-life balance. Women have led the call for more work-life balance, for example, often pathologizing work-centric people as "workaholic," evoking images of the addicted alcoholic. More work-life balance may yield greater net benefit to society although it must be acknowledged that working long hours can contribute to Gross World Flourishing, whether it's the accounts-payable clerk who wants to ensure that people get paid on time or the cardiologist who sees patients at nights and weekends, saving lives. In addition, important life-changing discoveries were, in part, the result of "workaholics," whether Jonas Salk who put in 70+ hour workweeks for years to develop the polio vaccine, the unsung heroes who long worked into the wee hours, developing Google-Search and the iPhone, or temporary "workaholics" like the team of bridge builders who, after the vital San Francisco Bay Bridge was destroyed in an earthquake, worked 16-hour days to rebuild that portal to and from San Francisco in just a few days rather than the government-estimated months.

Fewer scientists. The otherwise respected president of Harvard, Lawrence Summers, got fired for opining that more men that women may have the talent and predilection for science careers. Notwithstanding his having been fired for that, it may contain some truth, so a possible effect of a world without men could be fewer scientists or fewer excellent ones, whether in engineering, medicine, biotech, AI, or yes, developing even safer and more effective birth control. (FYI: Both the birth control pill and the tampon were developed by men.)

Monosexuality. A world without men would mean that women would have to choose among lesbianism, autoeroticism, and asexuality. Given the male/female tensions, which have accelerated in recent years, not to mention the 50% divorce rate, whether monosexuality is a net plus is an open question.

Tasks. While some women are good at and enjoy plumbing, roofing, and rat extermination, a world without men means that women must take on everything from home building to cleaning out the garage to the aforementioned rat extermination. Honey-do lists would be women's work.

My takeaway

Perhaps no surprise, I believe the world is better with both men and women. But as I said at the outset. I find it fun to contemplate extreme thought experiments if only to be reassured that the status quo ain't so bad. I hope you feel that way too.

A Telemarketer with a Soul

Jed never thought he'd be desperate enough to take a job as a telemarketer. After all, he has a college degree. He comes from a middle- class background. And he isn't bad looking.

With permission, 18/1 Graphics Studio

But despite the college's protestations about a liberal arts education's value, in terms of dollar value, it had been worth less than all those term papers students write that vanish into the ether.

Jed rationalized taking a telemarketing job in that it wasn't an extended warranty scam or non-existing but heartstring- pulling nonprofit. It was for of a legitimate charity, the ADHD Foundation.

The training was sophisticated: "Qualify the mark: Ask questions that hide your intent such as "What do you enjoy doing? If their answer is, for example, 'I love travel,' bingo, he's got money. If so, keep them on the phone long enough to build enough of a relationship and then make The Ask. Make it small for starters. You'll come back to them next week with an excuse for a bigger ask."

Jed's quota was standard for the telemarketing industry: 100 dials a day. Jed's first few dozen proceeded uneventfully. Yes, most hung up as soon as they heard the sound of the boiler room before Jed had even started his pitch. But he did reel in $740, three times his daily pay. So for today at least, he wasn't at risk of getting replaced by a person or robocaller.

Most people who spoke at all with him were older— Mainly old people pick up their phone, let alone say more than, "Sorry, I don't respond to telemarketers." Click.

Leah was not only younger sounding but, perhaps because she was lonely, pushed the conversation. After Jed said, "I'm with the ADHD Foundation," she said, "I'm not hyperactive but do have an attention deficit. I jump from idea to idea, thing to thing."

Jed smiled through the phone and, trained to keep her on the phone a while before making The Ask, he asked, "Leah (The training also stressed using the mark's name), what do you enjoy doing?" Her reply: "Right now, I don't have much time for enjoying. I'm a housekeeper at a motel, you know, clean 100 toilets a day?"

That reminded Jed that his 100 dials a day were nothing compared with her 100. So he decided to go off script, looking around to be sure his boss wouldn't overhear. And he thought, "The hell with the company's yield-per-hour metric." "Leah, I am supposed to ask you to donate money but really, it's okay. You sound nice. Would you like to tell me a little about yourself?"

They had a nice conversation. Alas that did get overheard by the telemarketer in the next cube, who ratted him out and Jed got fired. But he walked out happy, looking forward to coffee with Leah.

One Way to Get a Promotion

I'm one of the six directors in one of the federal agencies that deal with immigration. I was angry that two of my peers got promoted to senior director even though I know I'd do a far better job.

identity chris is, Flickr, CC 2.0

So when an opportunity arose to take a "creative" approach to getting that promotion, I took it. Let me explain.

A reporter from a major newspaper wanted to prove that our agency is anti-immigration — I could tell that was her slant from the questions she asked us.

Well, two days later, we had our usual private weekly meeting of the directors and senior directors. The presenter was the last remaining director who was appointed during the Trump administration. Not surprising, he argued that the pool of people who are willing to leave their homeland and illegally sneak into the U.S. are disproportionately people who have been unsuccessful in their homeland. He used a PowerPoint deck to support his position.

I realized that the reporter would find that deck a smoking gun. So I gave $100 to the overnight janitor to copy the deck onto a flash drive.

I am in favor of legalizing undocumented migrants so I would have given the flash drive to the reporter no matter what. But I figured it could help me get my promotion, and here's how I did it. I told her that I had a flash drive that would prove her contention that our agency was anti-illegal-immigration but that it was hard for me to get it so I'd only give it to her if she promised to praise me in her article.

And she did. Her "expose" called me "a beacon of progressivity, shining a light for the undocumented."

My boss, a fellow liberal, loved it and, in a month, I was promoted to senior director. Clever, huh?!

Kamal

It's ironic that Kamal was the one who had convinced Apex, the pharmaceutical giant, to partner with David Cohen, an Israeli inventor. It's not just that Kamal was the lowest-level person on Apex's strategic partnerships committee, nor that Kamal's parents had immigrated

With permission, 18/1 Studio

from Gaza, but also that Kamal had to decide whether to blow the whistle on the Israeli's behalf.

You see, Apex's strategic partnership team met today to discuss the excellent results from animal trials of Cohen's new injectable "virtual cartilage" that would eliminate the need for much hip replacement surgery.

Kamal was surprised that there was any objection to proceeding to human trials. It came from Apex's chief lobbyist who had requested to sit in on the meeting. The lobbyist sighed, "These days, giving Israel credit, even for a medical breakthrough is, let's just say, sensitive. Apex could pay a big price."

Kamal was shocked. Millions of people suffer so much pain from arthritis and if they're old or in poor health, hip replacement surgery is risky, not to mention expensive.

But Kamal was a mere midrange researcher and grateful to have a job paying $240,000 and that the job is at Apex— a source of pride to him and his family.

Kamal knew that he'd more likely get a sympathetic response from Israeli rather than American media, especially from the Jerusalem Post. He googled and found the email address of its editor-in-chief, and stared at it.

Jokester Janitor

I didn't become a janitor because I was stupid. It was when I heard of someone with a PhD who had to drive from college to college in the usual strangling traffic in what he called, "My Brainwashing Buggy" to teach one class per college to cobble together $50,000 a year, no benefits. At the same time, I heard that the city was hiring janitors at $62,000 to start, with tons of benefits. I'm not status conscious. I just wanted to make enough money to move out of my crazy parents' house. So I applied.

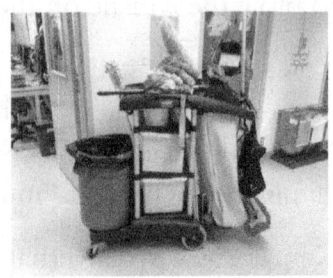

pxhere, free to use

I'm not happy as a janitor. But it isn't the reason people think—It's not boring. It's actually fun seeing executives' offices—what's on their walls, their bookshelves, and when they're not there, the papers on their desk. It's fun to see what they're working on—I get to see government bureaucracy up close without being a victim of it.

The problem is that in certain neighborhoods, some kids and even the occasional adult give us hell. As bad, at parties, saying I'm a janitor, let alone for the city, is a conversation stopper.

But I'm golden handcuffed—The good pay, lots of holidays and vacation days, health insurance, even a pension—Thank you, taxpayer!

So I can't quit but could I add some spice to my life? So I googled, "How to be a stand-up comedian" and soon I was doing open-mic nights as The Jokester Janitor.

That has provided the spice and, at parties, when they ask me what I do, I can say I'm a stand-up comedian—That's a conversation *starter*. When they ask if I can do a bit for them. I oblige, for example:

> I was looking for a new janitor job and was late for my job interview—I over*swept*. A few of my janitor friends formed a band, The *Bleach* Boys. When I got sick of being a janitor, I tried to get into NASCAR but they rejected me because my car went *broom broom*. So I got a job as a garbage man but was worried there was no training. The boss said, "You'll pick it up as you go." Now, how rich am I? *Filthy* rich.

The World's Kindest IRS Agent

The parishioners acted so Christian when Pastor John finished his homily and peered out at them in hopes of approval. Many of them nodded or smiled but John could tell that it was an act of charity. So on the walk home, John took the long way through the forest. He thought, "Deep down, I don't think I have the calling or maybe I've lost it."

Nick Youngson CC 3.0 Pix4free

John heard growling and yelping deeper into the woods and edged closer to sea—A dog fight had just ended.

Men were yelling, for example, "Yeah!" or "Fuck, you just cost me $50!" A man was dragging the losing, yelping dog, one of its legs hanging by ligaments and the man sneered, "Fucking loser!" and kicked the dog which then curled into a ball and the man kept dragging him away.

John plodded back to the road and thought of how many times he had preached that God has given man free will and that God works in mysterious ways. Now John wasn't sure he believed any of it. How could a loving God create such people? How could a loving God allow torturing innocent dogs?

In the seminary, John had been exposed mainly to Christian doctrine and in his search for answers now he decided to read Buddha's teachings. What made him stop reading was this quote: "Love what you're doing, work hard at it through your life, and you will have achieved true success."

John was comforted by its suggesting he didn't need to change. So he returned to his job unchanged but continued to feel that something is wrong.

One day after church, Thomas, a tired-looking parishioner in his early 60s asked Pastor John, "Can we talk?" And Thomas explained: "I was let go from my job and I've tried hard to find another one and no one wants me except for near minimum wage. My wife and I can't live on that and we can't afford to retire. We could live another 20, 30 years."

John asked, "Have you seen an accountant? Thomas replied, "I should but I'm scared to. He'll tell me I need to get another job which I can't or we could end up homeless."

"Thomas, would you tell me a little about your financial situation?" Fifteen minutes later, Thomas said, "That practical advice you just gave me did more to raise my spiritual spirits than, well…" and Pastor John waited. "Well, more even than church services". John's face dropped just a bit and felt that was final confirmation that indeed he did not have the calling.

After Thomas left, John got on his computer, looked up online accounting courses and took an introductory one then a second one and started a third but found that hard and so dropped it.

John occasionally slipped financial metaphors into his homilies and practical advice into his spiritual counseling but after more counseling with parishioners that felt of little help, John looked at the job listings for accountants. All of them required years of experience except one: The IRS, which just got $84 billion to hire new agents and so became lenient in its hiring criteria. Despite John's lack of the required accounting degree, he applied and the interviewer chose to hire him when John said, "It is a sin for people to cheat on their taxes. I'll do everything in my power for the government to get what it's legally entitled to."

As a pastor, John was all about kindness and forgiveness but he steeled himself to fulfill that promise. Indeed, John was a tough revenue agent, demanding documentation even for small items and insisting that each taxpayer pay every dollar that he had unearthed in the audit. As a result, in John's second month he won Revenue Agent of the Month for obtaining the most additional money.

But every day, John was returning from work sadder. Finally, one day, a sorry-looking person who was being audited without the usual accountant mouthpiece said that his house cleaner had thrown away all the tax receipts. And John decided to do a 180: He let the taxpayer go with minimum penalty and for the first time in a long time, John felt right with the world.

And for the rest of his life, John followed the Buddha's advice that he had read: Love what you're doing, work harder through your life, and you will have achieved true success And John decided that his work was to be the world's kindest IRS agent.

Chill Coaching

Shelley and I went to the same high school and I had a crush on her — She was pretty, smart, and convenient: She lived on my block. But I was too shy to ask her (or anyone) out. But I would lie in bed imagining, well, being with her.

SomatArt, DeviantArt, CC

We went off to different colleges and five years later, we both had graduated but back living with our parents.

Shelley and I took a walk and we admitted that neither of us felt very employable with our degrees from a middling college and me with my major in sociology, she in gender students. Even more embarrassing, neither of us were very motivated to work. We had been in school a long time and we agreed that while we were still young and our parents were willing to continue supporting us, we wanted to take more time to explore, figure out who we are and, okay, have more fun.

We also agreed that many college graduates and especially dropouts feel that way but were feeling guilty or just wanted their parents off their back. Shelley said, "Hey, what if we start Chill Coaching: one-on-ones and groups to help Gen Z'ers feel okay about who they are?"

I liked the idea and, in our chill way, we just asked our friends if they'd like to come to a free introductory meeting at my place. Six kids — oops, I mean young adults — showed up and we had fun. We talked about what we liked to do: travel, yoga, hiking, rock climbing, music, going to protests, and okay, partying, with all that implies. None of us were eager to "grow up" and get a grown-up job. Even being a barista seemed like a pain: Get up really early and then grind coffee and blend smoothies all day?

Chill Coaching took off and after a year, we were making enough to at least pay the minimum monthly payment on our student loans.

Today, we just finished a group session — It had the most attendees ever: 46! And Shelley and I sat down and over a beer, okay and some weed, and took a step back. I asked, "Hey, we're doing well and we're helping the next generation to be more chill." Shelly shrugged, "Is that really good?"

That's got me thinking.

Fantasy Traffic School

I got stopped by the highway patrol. "Do you know how fast you were going?"

"No sir."

"77 in a 65. I'll give you a break. I'll give you 75 in a 65."

I thought, "You should be nominated for sainthood," but just asked, "How much will it be?"

Jill Siegrist, Flickr, CC2.0

"You'll be notified by mail."

I put my head down and sighed.

It came in the mail all right: $515. Or, if I want to go to traffic school, a mere $380 plus the traffic school's $99 fee. That's almost 500 bucks but it doesn't go on your record so my insurance wouldn't go up.

I picked CarLoad of Laughs Traffic School and I'm glad I did.

Work Stories

I didn't think it would be a good choice. I showed up and there were a couple dozen other "violators" and an instructor who looked like he'd rather have a root canal.

He mumbled, "Okay. 6 hours and 45 minutes and you'll get your certificate. Let's get started. Your car must be how many feet behind a stopped school bus?" An eager beaver raised her hand, "20 feet."

The instructor buzzed like on a TV quiz show and said, "Far enough that you can't hear the kids' farting. Just kidding. You're right—20 feet."

"How does a cop know you've run a stop sign?" We were quick learners from the eager beaver's experience, so none of use raised our hand and he said, "You've *run* a stop sign if you *jog* past it." Only one person even bothered to groan. He said, "Just kidding. The cop sees if your wheels have completely stopped turning."

"Why shouldn't you speed? Cause you might get caught—500 bucks ka-chang. Seriously, you know why it's wrong to speed."

After 45 minutes of that, he said, "Let's take our first break."

He seemed the most eager to get out of the classroom. After a minute of commiseration with my fellow lawbreakers, I too wanted out of the stuffy room, so I wandered outside. Instead of hanging out with fellow scholars in the front of the building, I moped to the back—It's fun to see what we're not supposed to see—usually stuff like used oil from a restaurant or broken crockery from a plant store. But this time, I struck gold. There was our burnout instructor smoking a joint— Manna from heaven!

As soon as he saw me, he flung away the joint. I sauntered over, picked it up, smelled it to confirm and said, "Hmm, you needed a little something to try to make you funny?" He said, "Please, don't tell anyone."

I strutted back into the torture chamber, I mean classroom, where I told my classmates what I saw.

When the instructor returned, he acted like nothing had happened but I wasn't going to let that happen. I said, "So, Mr. Instructor, so you've decided to end the course right now and give us all our certificate of completion."

He said, "Huh?" whereupon I started chanting, "Weed. Weed. Weed. Cert. Cert. Cert. Weed. Weed. Weed. Cert. Cert. Cert." The students joined the chorus.

The final nail in his coffin was when I said, "Now, you don't want me to go to your company and tell them about your stoner break, do you? Like our tickets, it would go on your record—and that would cost more than a hike in your insurance."

From the paper bag on the floor next to his desk, the instructor grabbed the stack of certificates, slammed it onto his desk, and swayed out.

As soon as I got back in my car, I patted my certificate and made a point of—after checking for cops—rolling through a stop sign. My wheels definitely were turning. Ahh!"

Kansas to Vegas

In the Salina, Kansas church I grew up in, filled with well-wishers, my dad, Pastor Peter was at the altar, performing the most important wedding ceremony of his life: mine.

Tomas Del Cora, Wikimedia, CC2.0

With tears in his eyes, he whispered, "Mary, do you take Travis to be your lawfully wedded husband in sickness and in health, for richer, for poorer until death...

Before he could say "do us part," I ran out, ripped the "Just Married" sign off the back of our car, pulled Travis's suitcase out, left it on the sidewalk, and drove off.

I had no idea where I was headed. I just knew I had to get away from ordinary Kansas life, especially daughter-of-Kansas-preacher's life. I got on the Interstate and drove west. Except for pit stops, I drove straight through the Oklahoma panhandle, North Texas, and into New Mexico, where I saw a sign that felt like a *sign*: Albuquerque 212, Phoenix 520, Las Vegas 777. "777?!" and because Vegas is the opposite of ordinary Kansas, I had found my destination.

What was I going to do there? I have no skills. In Salina, I was just a waitress.

On arriving in Vegas, I knew I needed clothes and didn't want to run out of money. So my first stop was a Salvation Army store. I was so nervous, so many things going through my mind, that I forgot that I was still in my wedding dress! I only realized it when people started laughing at me.

So I grabbed the first dress that called to me, of all things, a gold-sequined cocktail dress: short, too short, and scoop neck, lots of cleavage would show, too much. But it sure is different than Kansas, pure Vegas, and for $5? I wasn't going to take the time to try it on. I wanted out of there, now!

I tried it on in the car and felt embarrassed that I loved it. It was a sign of my new life, the opposite of Salina.

I didn't expect to have to be spending much of my own money on my honeymoon, so I checked into a cheap hotel in a neighborhood I called "dicey"— perfect for Vegas. To avoid being seen in sequins, I raced up to my room.

I looked at myself in the mirror and thought, next stop, Wal-Mart, to get normal clothes. Then I asked myself, what am I going to do to make money?" More waitressing? I was tired of that. I'm here to do something new. Seeing my cleavage in the mirror, I laughed, hooker? Never! But I do look like a cocktail waitress— maybe at one of those famous Vegas hotels?

So after a good night's sleep, which I sure needed, I went to the fancy hotels I had heard of: Wynn's, the Venetian, and MGM Grand. All three came up snake-eyes. Or is it craps—I don't know gambling. I asked why they turned me down: "Is it my dress?" No, they loved my "get-up" but wanted to hire someone who had already been a cocktail waitress in Vegas.

They told me to try the Sahara, Circus-Circus, and even the Best Western. But I got the same answer and got scared.

Driving back to my hotel in its dicey neighborhood, I passed Winners Motel and Casino. Two of the letters in the neon sign were out. I thought, maybe you gotta start somewhere. Looking up and down my dress, the manager hired me.

I hated the job: The slot machines' nonstop noise and the players whose politeness sometimes faded into rudeness after their second drink. One guy said, "Baby, you probably make $15 an hour. How'd you like $200? Come to my room and I'll show you how."

I turned him down with a polite, "Thank you but I don't do that." But after my shift, back in my room, I started thinking. After all, my fiancée and yeah other guys said I was hot. And it would pay a lot better than Winners Motel and Casino. But what would my parents think, especially my father, preacher man!?

But the next morning, which for me was noon, on my phone, I went to the website of the only brothel I'd ever heard of: the Camara Ranch. It wanted applications for "courtesans." And without thinking about it much, I applied. I figured they'd never hire me— I definitely had no "prior experience working in a brothel." That *was* a question on the application. But the same day, I got a call for an interview. I wore my sequin dress and they hired me subject to passing the blood test and criminal background check. In the meantime, they gave me a training booklet, including how to do a "dick check:" looking for STDs.

Two days later, they called and asked if I'd sign a 14-day contract at $1,000 a day— live-in. I signed but soon broke the contract. It was the very first guy. I didn't get beyond the few minutes of "warm-him-up conversation" when I cried, "I can't do this." And as I did at the altar, I ran out and drove back to Salina.

As soon as I got home, my parents cried, I cried, and of course, I apologized. Next, I saw Travis and swore on a stack of Bibles that I'd never run away again. But he said, "I can't count on you, Mary. No."

As I'm writing this, I'm back to waitressing and wondering if, like my fellow Kansan, Dorothy in the Wizard of Oz, maybe there really is no place like home. I'm not sure.

Sam's Last Concert

In the wings, Sam could hear the concertmaster tuning up the orchestra.

With permission, 18/1 Graphics Studio

"Damn, my hand is shaking more than usual—It's a bad Parkinson's day. Plus, it's my last concert—I'm nervous. Glad I decided on the Grieg, but with these hands, nothing's easy."

Work Stories

Sam had been a concert pianist his whole life. At age 11, he finished 4th in the Midwest Regional Young Artists Competition and now at 83, had performed 45 concerts, including one with the Kansas City Symphony. He thought,

True, that was just in the K.C. Symphony's summer festival when lots of the A players were on vacation but still...Somehow, I wish my ex-wife were here. How could she have dumped me? I still wish she were here tonight...Do I play it safe? A lot of note mistakes would make the audience think I stayed at it too long, like those star baseball players who'd rather hit .200 than retire. Or do I go for a home run, a chance at a write-up in the Kansas City Star: "Roseman finishes with a flourish!"

The conductor gave Sam a forced smile and Sam strode on stage.

"This is it. Deep breaths, deep breaths. Damn, my hands are shaking more. I'm taking too long. I gotta get out there. Stand up straight. Old men hunch. Stride, don't shuffle."

But Sam could manage only to shuffle on stage. He hung onto the piano with one hand as he bowed his head to the audience. "If I tried to bow from the waist, I could fall."

And he sat down at the piano. "I've had this moment so many times but this is different."

Sam used his old trick of adjusting the seat up and then back down again, not because it needed adjusting but to buy a little more time to ground himself before the moment of truth.

And Sam began and took every reasonable risk he could—and most of the time he won. Yes, his boldness caused a few note mistakes but only the ignorant or meanspirited could criticize his exciting performance. It was inspiring at any age but for an 83-year-old with advanced Parkinson's?! It gives me the chills just to tell you about it.

And yes, Sam got not just the usual obligatory extended applause, bestowed as much to protest classical music's dying popularity as to acknowledge the performer, but fervent applause and then, yes, a standing ovation. Not a charity ovation, a heartfelt one. And Sam, who usually was too shy to look at the applauding audience and so would stare at the back wall, soaked in the smiling, standing people. Then he sighed and plodded off stage for what he thought was the last time.

Sam shuffled into his dressing room, closed the door, and dropped into a chair. "I survived. I didn't embarrass myself, but I can't go to the reception—That's like a retirement party, where everyone tries to make light of it being the beginning of the end, my end."

There was a knock on the door. 'Daddy?" His daughter opened the door and gushed, "You were amazing. You were really amazing! Come on. They're all waiting for you."

Sam knew there was no avoiding it, so he trudged downstairs. When he arrived, the chatter morphed into

Work Stories

applause. He thought, "No one likes long speeches, and nothing ungracious, I should be a good boy." But he couldn't resist saying what he really felt. "Honestly, I can't stand the thought that this will be my last performance." And he teared up.

A four-year-old toddled up to him: "Do you want to play in my class?" And Sam Roseman went on to play more concerts than he had in his entire life-in preschools and elementary schools, first just locally, then around the country. He never got paid, indeed had to pay his travel expenses but didn't begrudge it: "I can't think of a better way to spend my money than to teach young kids to love classical music and that old people aren't necessarily irrelevant."

A Therapist Support Group

I was feeling burned out as a psychotherapist so I figured I'd try a support group for therapists. It felt particularly opportune because it was the group's first meeting.

IgorVetushko, CC, Courtesy Deposit Photos

But as soon as they started talking, I felt like a loser. They were speaking so confidently:

"Yes, I got great results with EMDR (eye-movement desensitization and reprocessing."

"My modality of choice has become dialectic behavior therapy."

"An eclectic mix of trauma-informed, mindfulness-based, and neo-Freudian feminist paradigms is working well."

I've tried many of those and my clients say they like and respect me, but too many continue to have problems or, as they train us to say, "challenges" or "areas for growth." What has really gotten to me was when a client said, "I've gotten insight but my life is no better, while my wallet is much thinner."

But after those therapists had done their peacock preening, they began to open up, although just a crack: "I'm glad to be here because, not matter how successful, we all can grow. "I am having just a bit of a challenge with just a few of my clients, especially those long-term, treatment-resistant, major depression."

I decided to blurt it out. "To tell you the truth, I'm having a helluva time even with most of my garden-variety, self-absorbed neurotics. And one time, when I actually fell asleep during a phone session, at the end, the client said, "Dr. Weller, this was our most effective session. Thank you so much. I feel like you listen so well. I felt really heard."

As I drove home, I was reminded that therapists can get a job working for Medicare, where they don't have to see clients, just screen which ones the taxpayer should spring for another round of sessions. I think I could do that job well.

Trying

Even since a vet came to my high school biology class, I wanted to be a vet. but when I got to college, those hard science courses convinced me I wasn't smart enough. Fortunately, with taxpayer help, I figured I could make enough money as a vet-tech.

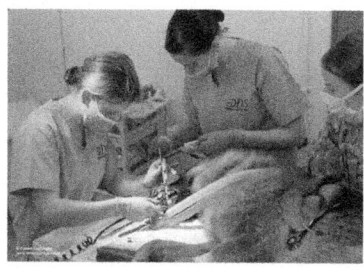
Defence Imagery, Flickr, CC 2.0

I got hired by a local vet and quickly got more and more responsibility. I started just by taking notes but soon got to draw blood and then to assist in surgery.

The vet did many successful surgeries but one time, a buffed, tattooed man brought in a dog that had been mauled in a dog fight. The doctor had to fix deep gashes, her hand slipped, and cut a nerve. When the dog woke, he couldn't walk well at all — He collapsed after just a few steps. The vet was mad at herself and asked me whether I thought she should put the dog down and just tell the dog-fighter owner that the dog died unavoidably in surgery. I felt I should leave the decision to her, so I just said, "It's a personal decision. Do what you think is wise."

She decided to tell the owner that his dog would never walk again and the owner said, "No biggie. Finish him."

I couldn't live with that so I asked the vet if I could adopt the dog. She advised against it: "It would be too difficult, for you and for the dog." *She was right* — I couldn't get even get him to go out to "do his business."

I asked the vet if I could be the one to put the dog down. She nodded and, my hand shaking, I gave the injection and cried.

I think I'm going to try again to do pre-vet.

A Perfectionist Conductor

Joel, the new conductor, wouldn't let the orchestra get past even the first four notes. It was their first rehearsal of Beethoven's 5th and Andra, one of the violinists sighed, "Joel, or should I say, Maestro, this isn't the New York Phil. It's the fucking Oakwood Community Chamber Orchestra. Chill!"

Pix4Free Free to use

Joel said, "You chill. No, on second thought, you're fired." and Joel thought, "This is the New America: Just be, whatever. It's cool."

Andra scoffed, "I don't know if I can survive without the zero income of this volunteer gig." And she sashayed out.

That got Joel even more perfectionistic: "Most orchestras— including the New York Phil— play the 5th first three notes at the same volume. It's more powerful to make each note a bit softer, starting with fortissimo and ending at barely forte. Then play that shocking fourth note, and play it fortissimo. And thus we will have

Work Stories

appropriately presaged the entire first movement. Let's try it."

Joel's anger with Andra, indeed if he was honest— with a number of the players' veneration of "good enough"— made him change the program to the most challenging ever: Ravel's Pavane for a Dead Princess, Tchaikovsky's 6th Symphony, and Rachmaninoff's 3rd Piano Concerto, having recruited, no, implored, a wonderful pianist to do it. Joel knew the orchestra association didn't have the money so, out of his own pocket, he paid her $1,000 plus expenses, plus the cost to rent the oddball piano she liked to play: a Kawai KG-7D.

Joel and most of the musicians were gratified by the performance, feeling that all the work was worth it, allowing them to achieve well beyond what they thought they could. A few said they got goosebumps.

But when Joel asked the president of the orchestra association how the audience reaction compared with the previous conductor's concerts, her answer: "About the same."

So Joel quit the conductorship and turned his attention to preparing for a solo piano concert: Chopin's Ballade #1, Beethoven's Appassionata Sonata, Liszt's Hungarian Rhapsody #4, and his favorite work: Ravel's devilish Gaspard de La Nuit.

But while rehearsing just two weeks before the performance, Joel thought, "They're right. This is all stupid." And he canceled his performance, asked the president of the Oakwood Community Chamber

Orchestra for his old job back, and promised to have a new, fun attitude.

Faith Shaken

The pastor sat in the parish house preparing his sermon. Like most clerics, he occasionally had a crisis of faith but found it easier to minister by not focusing on that, especially when sermonizing: A major purpose of the church is to comfort the faithful, and expressing doubt rarely does that.

With permission, 18/1 Graphics Studio

So the pastor decided to give his sermon on how God comforts even when inexplicably bad things happen.

He began, "We are all understandably shaken by what's happening to the poor people of Ukraine. How could an omnipotent, loving God allow that? We find an answer in Scripture. I read from Philippians 4:6-7:

> *Do not be anxious about anything, but in every situation, by prayer and petition, with thanksgiving, present your requests to God. And the peace of God, which transcends all understanding, will guard your hearts and your minds in Christ Jesus.*

So, dear parishioners ...

At that moment, the church shook. Fortunately, the earthquake caused only minor damage. But that raised the doubts about a loving, omnipotent God in at least a few parishioners and yes, in the pastor.

He then had to decide whether greater good would accrue if, in continuing the sermon, acknowledging his doubt? Or would he be wiser to express gratitude for God sparing the church from greater harm?

What would you do?

Reduction

Dominique couldn't allow herself to doubt her decision. After all, she had paid so many dues: expensive culinary school, "sous chef" (mainly a soup stirrer), associate chef at a mid-range restaurant, and finally, executive chef there—Her dream come true.

With permission, 18/1 Graphics Studio

But slowly, Dominique couldn't suppress her doubts. Even being the head chef got boring— You had to make the same dishes again and again.

Because she had to work nights and weekends, her social life consisted mainly of hanging out with the restaurant staff after the last customers had left.

Most dispiriting was the pretense: Does bocuf tournedos with a balsamic reduction really taste that much better than a good burger even if they were the same price, which they definitely are not?

But what put Dominique over the edge was when a waiter tossed back a part-eaten plate: "Table 17 says he wanted his quail medium-rare and this is medium."

Back at her apartment, Dominique told the quail story to her roommate who was a waiter at Hash House, a basic breakfast joint. He responded, "Our customers would never send your food back and my boss would hire you in a minute. She's trying to upgrade the image to appeal to the middle class. She'd treat you like a queen. Just talk to her."

Because it was a breakfast place, Dominique would be off at noon and so could have a normal social life. So she agreed to try it.

But working with frozen hash brown patties, powdered eggs, and Cost-Rite Pancake and Waffle Mix felt like a violation of all she had committed to.

She was also frustrated by the sous chefs so often calling in sick, and in those cases, Dominique had to go back to being the soup stirrer.

So after one day at Hash House, she wondered whether she should search for another dream.

Double Promotion

"Sandy, you've done all I've asked and more. we really need you in Detroit. So I'm giving you a double promotion: You're currently a manager. I'm going to jump you over director and make you a VP, which means a $100,000 pay increase. You'll spend a year in Detroit and then, if you wish, we'll transfer you back here. What do you say?"

With permission, 18/1 Graphics Studio

I couldn't believe my reaction. Yes, there was some fear but mainly, I just didn't want more responsibility. It would mean more hours, more pressure, and living in Detroit? Even the $100,000 didn't move me: That would be taxed at my top rate so I'd be lucky to net half that.

But if I turned it down, I'll be seen as the stereotype, committed more to family and personal life than to work. Will I be forever stuck at the manager level? Do I even want a higher level? Could they lay me off and then, I might not even get as good a job?

I turned it down and walked out of my boss's office feeling good. But my family and friends called me from lazy. insecure, a BS feminist: "You rail about a pay gap and then you turn down $100,000 more?!"

Maybe I should take the job. Do you think he'll let me? Or will he think I'm too wishy-washy?

I'm going to walk the dog.

The Hope Giver

I was an oncologist and felt burned out from giving bad news. "I'm sorry, it's Stage 4. We could try another round of chemo but…"

With permission, 18/1 Graphics Studio

When I began as an oncologist, my patients thought I was unusually caring, taking plenty of time, "guidelines" be damned. I cared so much that when a patient left the exam room, I often crept to my office, closed the door, and cried. I usually came home drained and eventually, to dull my sadness, succumbed to an occasional Vicodin.

But over time, to insulate myself further from the pain, I became briefer, more distant, and eventually even cold, especially if the patient was asking what I thought were dumb questions.

Patients complained to the head of my practice and, finally, I was let go: "You need a break."

But at age 64, I didn't have the drive to look hard for another job, let alone to start a solo practice. So I made only desultory efforts, sort of retiring without officially telling that to anyone even to myself.

After a few months of trying to stay busy with reading, hiking, and binge-watching, I was feeling bereft, useless.

Then, one day, when I was feeling particularly sorry for myself, sitting in an outdoor cafe. I noticed a woman reading a book on job hunting.

I didn't want to reveal that I too could use a job. That could be disheartening to her and embarrassing to me, so I asked, "Getting anything from the book?"

She said, "I guess, maybe a little hope, but it feels a little empty, like motivational-speaker overoptimism: "Each and every one of you can do it!" Her face dropped just slightly, like she was trying to hide her despondency, like I was.

Wanting to give her realistic hope like I used to do with my early patients, I offered a couple possibilities, hoping she'd latch onto one: "In addition to a cover letter, do you want to try including a one-pager about your philosophy of work or how you'd tackle the job? Or how about making your LinkedIn profile specific to the kind of work you'd most enjoy? That way, you'd stand out to that employer looking for that needle in a haystack."

"I like that last idea.," she said. "I'd love to write catalog copy for a gardening company, you know, seeds, plants, supplies."

A little embarrassed but feeling good, I said, "I gotta go. Good luck."

But as I walked away, I realized that giving her hope, realistic hope, gave me pleasure while giving people something they desperately need.

So I kept my eye out for opportunities to give people realistic hope: my friend who was taking longer than expected to recover from an injury, my other friend who so wanted to meet Mr. Right, my father who was increasingly sad as he faced mortality.

All that felt good but I felt an urge to do something bigger. But for months, nothing came to me. Then, I was listening to a podcast urging kids to learn to code software, both for jobs of the future and to improve critical thinking.

Without thinking about it much, I bought 100 older-generation but still fine iPhones (90% less expensive than the current models), loaded it with great beginner, intermediate, and advanced interactive courses on how to code, visited high school classrooms in rural India, and gave a few phones to each teacher to give to students who'd likely make the most of those coding tutorials.

I have no idea how much good that did but I returned home feeling, well, hope.

"It's Not My Job to Make You Coffee"

"Martelle, I'm swamped. Would you make me coffee?"

Trying not to sound angry, Martelle said, "Michael, you know it's not my job to make you coffee. I'm your administrative assistant. That

TrentSD, Flickr, CC2.0

Work Stories

means Word docs, scheduling, and screening your email. It doesn't make me your maid."

"Never mind." Michael tried to say it evenly but it came out angry. He thought, "You're marginal, Martelle. I'd fire you except that it would be so difficult."

It's understandable that Martelle refused. After all, her mother *was* a maid and proud that Martelle had gotten Microsoft-certified in Word, PowerPoint, and even Excel. Plus, the media had endlessly told Martelle that BIPOCs are marginalized. In her mother's words, "When you face injustice, you must stand up if not rise up."

It's also understandable that Michael would have liked to fire Martelle. Especially when HR and other bosses stress collaboration, it doesn't seem like much, when he's busy, to ask his admin to make him a cup of coffee. Indeed Michael, despite his master's in computer science from CalTech, sometimes has to do tasks that a high school dropout could do. And Michael's views had roots deeper than colleges and media. His father was an engineer who believed in, "Unless you're sick, no excuses. Just get it done."

But Martelle had had enough. This wasn't the first time Michael "asked" her to make coffee. Worse, when she made a mistake, he'd often sigh condescendingly. And although she hadn't had a pay increase in 18 months, he turned her down, indeed hinted that she might have to accept a pay cut. She documented all that and filed a grievance with her union, which in turn, sent it to HR and to the EEOC, demanding a hearing.

When Michael saw the complaint, he quit and became a self-employed app developer. He's working on a better approach to matching job seekers with employers.

Thoughts in Class

Travis, a 5th grader: The teacher's bra strap always sticks out.

Teacher: I can't believe that Travis has already forgotten how to graph a parabola.

RDNE Stock project, Pexels, CC

Travis: She has big tits.

Teacher: I'm getting my period but I have to be good: Breathe, smile, teach.

Travis: I think Cheryl is starting to get tits.

Teacher: How in the world can I teach stupid, average, and smart kids in the same class?

Travis: I wonder if she'll ever catch me sticking gum under my desk.

Teacher: Travis is spacing out again. Oh, who cares?

Travis: It's fun to look at my watch and count the seconds until recess.

Teacher: It's fun to look at the clock and count the seconds until recess.

Travis: The bell's going to ring. Thank God!

Teacher: The bell's going to ring Thank God!

Robin Hood, The Meter Man

For Gavin, the perfect career was meter man: He liked redistributing from the rich to the government and, in turn, to the poor.

With permission, 18/1 Graphics Studio

On his ticket printer, he placed a label with tiny letters that only he could see: "I am Robin Hood, the King. I decide who gets taxed."

So he'd give a pass to beater cars but dare a Mercedes be in a red zone? $500, ka-chang. A Beemer's meter about to expire? To not lose an opportunity, Gavin would start writing the ticket a minute early, so when the meter expired, he could immediately press print.

If Gavin saw the owner approach, after putting the ticket on the windshield, he wouldn't walk away. He wanted to enjoy the owner's reaction, for example, "I came to put more money in the meter right on time. Damn! Please void that?" Officiously, Gavin would intone, "I am sorry. It's too late." Those were his favorite moments.

Gavin also was happy each time the government increased parking fines, which it often did. Last week, he attended the public hearing, which was placed in the penultimate spot in a long agenda— Politicians want the money but don't want to be associated with tax increases, let alone parking ticket increases.

When the council would pass the increase, which it always did, Gavin was probably the only person who was happy: More taxation power for Robin Hood. Now, an expired parking meter will be $99, double parking $199, too close to the intersection $299, hydrant $399, and red zone, the jackpot: $599.

Some of Gavin's motivation came from his liberal worldview but more foundational, it was his way of getting back at humankind, which had rejected him again and again. That started as a child when he was his classmates' resident punching bag. It continued through college, where he was shunned by girls, professors, even activist groups.

Gavin's anger increased over time and finally, when he was sure no one was looking, he'd let the air out of fat cats' tires: "Giving them a ticket and a flat tire. Helluva one-two punch!"

Gavin never had a moment of regret. And on his deathbed in the hospital, no one came to visit him. He was glad of that and his last words were to the nurse: "Just leave me alone."

Sowing Oats

In North Uist, one of Scotland's gale-swept North Isles, a few people farm black oats. That's one of the few things that will grow there, if you know what you're doing.

With permission, 18/1 Graphics Studio

Sandy MacTavish does. His family has been farming it for 15 generations. And at 35, Sandy was at the peak balance of energy and experience.

Olivia Jones had not been oat farming for 15 generations or even 15 minutes. After her divorce from her husband in London, she decided to, within the UK, get as far away as possible. Based merely on Google searches, she decided to move to North Uist, grow black oats, notable not just for the grain but because it produces good straw for baskets and chair backs.

She planted the oats in the April 1 to May 15 window and the seeds germinated well. But then, the plants started to yellow. A Google search didn't help— It said the problem usually is overwatering, underwatering, or a manganese or copper deficiency, but she tried those to no avail. She wondered if she needed to return to London, tail between her legs.

At the market, the isolated area's core, she asked a wise-appearing clerk who might help. He said, "Sandy MacTavish is your man."

One look at her plants and Sandy said, "No need for a soil test. Ya need more zinc. Use seaweed. Here, I'll give ya some. If your plants aren't green and growin' in two weeks, I'll make ya dinner."

But the plants did get green and growin', as were Olivia's spirits. She pictured giving her first basket to Sandy and cashing her first check from the mill.

She also pictured what it might be like to have dinner with Sandy. So, she said to him, "Well, turnabout's fair play. You won your bet, so I should make you dinner."

But in the directness that comes from living in North Isles' weather, Sandy said, "Miss Jones, that's very kind of ya but thinking of all my past says, I'm better off married just to my oats."

Unseen

Sara folded each turkey slice so it made an elegant, gentle hill. Yet she was quick enough that neither customers nor boss complained that she was slow. Indeed, she had gotten consistent raises in the year she was the sandwich maker at Sam's Sandwiches. She thought she'd just do it for a few months until she found a real job, but you know how inertia is.

With permission, 18/1 Graphics Studio

At 1:30, the lunch crowd was gone, so it was time for Sara to take her lunch. As usual, she walked the neighborhood but this day, sipping coffee as she walked, her caffeinated brain was particularly active.

She passed this guy who reminded her of someone she had dated. She cringed and thought, "I was so bad in bed."

She passed a boutique. The price tags of the dresses in the window were hidden. Looking at one that was particularly understated, she thought, "It looks like a rag. I wouldn't wear it if they paid me. Fat chance for me to be a model at size 12."

Sara passed a church and thought, "I would like to believe in God, in a hereafter, but I can't. There's too much bad luck in the world for there to be a loving, knowing God. I think man created the idea of God as a comfort when nothing else can comfort."

Then there were thoughts triggered merely by random passersby: "Am I glad to be anonymous, unseen, or do I hope someone recognizes me?"

Then she saw a telephone pole, a Tower of Babel hawking diverse events and causes. One caught her eye: "See Now: Free cataract surgery for children in need." She thought, "I thought only old people needed cataract surgery. My mom had it and it restored her life. Imagine a child whose parents couldn't afford the surgery." She wrote the telephone number.

At Sara's next break, she called and was invited to come watch a surgery. It was a 4-year-old with a nervous mother holding his hand as he lay on the operating table in a makeshift clinic in a gritty part of the city.

As the child sat up and immediately could see better, the nurse saw Sara crying in joy. After the patient and mom had left, they talked and the nurse asked if Sara would like to volunteer to help set up and clean up the operating room after a patient. She cried again.

She loved volunteering. She used the detail-orientedness of her sandwich-making to make the operating room just right for the doctor, nurse, and especially the patients.

Sara is still at Sam's Sandwiches but is taking night courses to become a surgical technologist.

Recipes from the IRS

I was a manager at the IRS. Yes, I recognize that it's right to collect as much taxpayer money as is legal, but after 23 years, it was tiring. And impatient by nature, I found myself getting ever shorter with my revenue agents. Flogging, whether of agents or taxpayers, is draining. So I retired early.

Nick Youngson, Pix4Free, CC 3.0

Still in my '50s, I wanted to stay busy. First, I considered going to the other side of the table—representing taxpayers in audits—but decided I wanted out of that world. I also wanted something not too—pardon the pun—taxing. Third, I wanted my interactions brief—I make a decent first impression but don't wear well.

So I decided to try to get a job as a supermarket checker. I was afraid it would be boring so, in the job interviews, I said I'd take the job only if I'd be allowed to hand out recipes based on what was in the shopper's cart. The supermarket chains said no—They were afraid that other checkers would complain to the union about unequal treatment, that it might become expected that everyone had to do something special.

But a family-owned grocery store said yes, perhaps because they were at risk of going out of business—The chains have larger selection and, because of economies of scale, lower prices.

What sealed the deal was when I explained that, as an IRS agent, I was good at detecting dishonesty, so I'd be vigilant against such stunts as hiding an expensive item in their cart under a big, heavy, cheap item like a sack of dog food that clerks scan without taking it out of the cart.

After some trial and error, I found that customers most appreciated not frou-frou recipes but easy, tasty ones for comfort food: burgers, mac and cheese, apple pie, and surprising to me, my salad recipe: "Any ol' lettuce, blue cheese, tomato, and Good Seasons Italian dressing."

The owner got so many compliments that he had me do a *Daily Demo*. He put the week's schedule on a blackboard in the front window.

A few weeks later, another checker, Alice, asked, "Have you thought about trying to get a cooking show on TV?" I replied, "There already are a zillion cooking shows—

Every time I turn on PBS, there's someone making some frou-frou thing: Elite Italian, Elegant Mexican, Thai to Die For." She said, "What's missing are the basics, the recipes you say your customers like best—easy comfort food. PBS may say no but how about a regular channel? I have no experience as a promoter but I do have a big mouth. Mind if I call around?" I was flattered, and I liked her style.

Six months later, on a local channel, I had a weekly show: *Recipes From the IRS*. IRS agents have emailed me praise and a few even said they were jealous. Oh, and I've started dating Alice.

The Carpenter

Your honor, before sentencing my husband, thank you for allowing me to speak on his behalf. I don't believe you've heard the whole story.

The judge nodded and here's what I said.

Marie Anna Lee, CC

Javier didn't want to be a criminal
and sneak in illegally, so he had to wait four years.

I met him here in the U.S. He was a student in my English-as-a-Second-Language class. Because he is a good carpenter, he was making $30 an hour, enough to support me and, after we got married, our daughter.

But illegal immigration has flooded the market, so my husband's pay kept going down. Eventually, all he could get was just-above minimum wage. And finally, sometimes he couldn't even get that.

And when I got pregnant with my second child, we talked about abortion because we couldn't afford another child, but we're Catholic, so we decided that God would provide.

Javier got more and more worried, then depressed, and started drinking. He always had liked a glass of wine when he came home from work but, little by little, it became two glasses, then two big glasses, then a half bottle. Then he started with tequila. And after so long without work — even when he went to the Home Depot parking lot where the illegals hang out waiting for jobs — he started drinking in the morning.

Well, on *the* morning, there he was at Home Depot, with his tool belt on so he looked professional, when one of the men called him gay for wearing it. Well, that was the last straw. He had been drinking that morning and he pulled the hammer from his tool belt, and in the culmination of all his frustration, slammed the guy in the head and the man died. I am hoping, your honor, that you'll take all this into consideration as you decide whether to send him to jail for the rest of his life.

The judge sentenced Javier to 25 years with possibility of parole in 20.

Dear reader, if you were Javier, what might you say to the illegals who were about to cross the border into the U.S?

The Warehouse Pairer

I wished someone had told me the simple truth that science courses are harder than others. That would have changed my life.

Defense Visual Information Distribution Service, Public Domain

You see, my first semester at college, I got an A in everything but struggled to a B in Intro to Biology for majors. So I changed my major to sociology. After I got my degree, I couldn't land a job except for two. The first was Lyft driver, which I didn't want because after car expenses, you make almost nothing. The other was as a warehouseman for a big company — dead-end. Best case, I'd be plucked as the one in 20 to supervise warehouse workers.

In the course of telling my biology-course story to my lunchpail buddies, I came up with an idea: How about we all chip in to hire some programmer to create an app that would be like Match.com but for pairing-up mentors and proteges. I contributed $250 and the other three each did 50 bucks, and we posted an ad on a site for programmers, explaining we weren't in it for the money but needed a programmer who'd do it for the love or for $400. And we found one — probably not the greatest programmer, but the perfect is the enemy of the good.

Fast-forward a few months and we launched YourMentoringMatch.com. It felt great that everyone now called me the Warehouse Pairer. But how would we populate it? We just started with friends and family and within a month, we had paired three mentors with three proteges. We then pitched our company's foundation, which agreed to have its programmers — aces — make the site really hum.

Who would have thought that getting a B instead of an A in a course would have had such a silver lining? Oh, and I've been promoted to the corporate office — I'm now a management trainee! And everyone still calls me the Warehouse Pairer.

Advanced Objections Training

I had met my quota for two quarters in a row, so I got promoted to senior development (fundraising) officer and was required to attend Advanced Objections Training. You see, most prospects ask few questions, mainly simple ones like, "Can my money go to the Dept of Psychology?" and they're satisfied with reductionistic but reassuring answers like, "Yes." So Basic Objections Training is enough.

Richard Hurd, CC 3.0

But a few prospects, usually fat cats, ask harder questions, so we get trained on what to say. I thought you might be curious to see the handout they gave us:

Advanced Donor/Prospect Objections and Model Answers

Prospective donor: Even though Fermat University is private, it gets lots of money from the taxpayer: student aid, research money, overhead. Why do you need my hard-earned money?

Your model answer: Good question. *(Use such praise often.)* We don't get enough from the government. Your money is crucial to supporting quality education, for example *(Insert the donor's hot button from their dossier, for example, first-generation college students.)*

Prospective donor: If my money goes for a scholarship, that rarely helps a kid go to college who otherwise wouldn't. Doesn't it merely substitute my money for the taxpayer's or what's already in your coffers, like your billion-dollar endowment?

Your model answer: Another good question. Your money usually enables us to offer students cash instead of loan. *(If that doesn't satisfy a potential five-figure donor, refer him or her to the assistant director of development.)*

Prospective donor: Studies find that many students grow little if at all http://tinyurl.com/36kbdadp in crucial benefits of a college education: writing and critical thinking. Aren't there more effective charities than universities, for example, a mentoring program for low-income gifted kids?

Your model answer: Of course, there are many good causes but giving to your alma mater does sow the seeds for excellence in launching our graduates' lives as well as support research that can improve lives. *(NB: Again, if* *your answer doesn't at least mollify a potential five-figure donor, offer to get a more detailed answer for them.)*

Prospective donor: But isn't your #1 mission theoretical research: four-dimensional mathematical space, the physics of sub-atomic particles, the 1,000th interpretation of Ulysses, the vast majority of which is extremely unlikely to yield practical application?

Your model answer: We can't know in advance what will yield practical application. Besides, isn't there beauty in understanding life's basics, the magnificence of everything from a leaf to literature? *(If that doesn't satisfy the prospect, it usually requires a deep conversation that's beyond what most donors find too complex to explore, especially with a fundraiser.)*

Prospective donor: When you say you'll match my money, it implies you'll *add* additional money to match mine. In fact, don't you usually just "match" by *listing* my money alongside what's already in your coffers?

Your model answer: It depends on the situation. If you like, I can check out whether that would apply to your donation. How much were you thinking of giving? *(If indeed, the prospect will only donate if we add funds, we can do that, but few donors insist on that.)*

Prospective donor: If I earmark money for a specific purpose, say the research on the foundations of cognition, the university knows that few donors check. How can I guarantee that my donation is used for that purpose?

Your model answer: We are an open book. Feel free to check in with any professor. *(Few do — Even most wealthy people are intimidated by PhDs.)*

NB: *If the donor says "I'll think about it," our research finds that 77.2% of the time, the donor doesn't donate. The good news is that a kindly follow-up call or email (Check the prospect's dossier for which one) simply asking, "Just calling to follow up on our good conversation and your great questions. Anything I can answer for you or do for you?" 41.3% of the time, that yields an immediate commitment and within a month, an additional 12.1%. So follow up!*

A Cheese Clerk Talks to His Dog

Raw Pixel, CC

I have a bachelor's degree, so I feel embarrassed to tell people I'm happy being a clerk at the cheese counter in a supermarket.

But I like to process things, and not just cheese. So today, I talked with my dog, Cheddar, about why I like it, why I'm not ambitious like everyone else.

Dear Cheddar, most of my friends don't like their job. Usually, they say they're putting up with crap because they feel they have to pay dues before getting a good job. But I know a lot of older people with "good" jobs who are overworked, underpaid, stressed, or feel they're not making much difference.

My job isn't just low-stress. It's not just that the hours are regular — No one's going to call me at home to say they need a brie. I satisfy nearly every customer — We sell good cheeses at a fair price. And I get to give out free samples. Everyone loves getting a freebie and I like giving them.

The pay's not great but with a roommate, I can make it.

The only thing I gotta watch out for is eating too much cheese. A little is fine but…

So, dear Cheddar, do you think I'm fooling myself and sooner than later, I'll want a "real" career but won't be hireable because who'd want to hire a cheese clerk?

I dunno but, in the meantime, Cheddar, how about a belly rub?

A Magical Teacher

I was one of the many kids who was more interested in magic than in school. So, instead of doing my homework, I often practiced magic tricks. It was fun and made me popular.

kidsmagic, CC

As an adult, while I couldn't make a living as a magician, I made a few bucks on the side doing magic at kids' birthday parties.

One time, I decided to try an experiment. Instead of just going for oohs and aahs, after a few of the illusions, I'd reveal the trick and offer a life lesson.

For example, after making solid steel rings appear to link together, I revealed that one of the rings is a *key ring*, which has an opening big enough for another ring to go into it. By hiding the opening in my palm, I can make it appear that solid is going through solid. The lesson: "If someone says or shows you something that seems untrue, it probably is. And not just kids get scammed, but grownups, for example, getting a call saying, "You've just won a million dollars!" If you actually entered the contest and won, you wouldn't be asked to pay anything to get the prize nor be asked to give any personal information or log into a website.

Then I did a trick in which, while talking, I pulled 25-feet of multicolored paper chain from my mouth. I then showed them that it was very thin paper coiled into a packet so small it can be hidden in your cheek and with practice, you can talk normally. The lesson: When you can't find something, could it be hidden somewhere? For example, when you can't find that piece of paper you need to bring back to school, like your homework or that note signed by your parent, where could it be hidden? Buried at the bottom of your backpack? Under some books in your room? In your dog's stomach?

They Tried to Get Rid of Me

I admit it, I'm an outspoken know-it-all, don't suffer fools gladly, and, like famed GE CEO Jack Welch, am not shy about firing weak employees. As a result, I've gotten shareholders a solid return and have taken our products from *Consumer Reports'* bottom ranks to top-rated. But that didn't matter to two of my three supervisees. Let me tell you what happened.

FreeRange, CC

One of the three, Laura, the one who likes me, told me that the other two were going to try to get rid of me. At a recent meeting of the three (I wasn't there), they were bad-mouthing me as usual and Laura decided to use her phone to record it, keeping it in her purse so no one saw. She played the operative part for me— They too were going to use a recording: "Let's bait the asshole. I'll keep my phone in my pocket, press record, and bait him to say something homophobic, sexist, and racist. If we get juicy clips, we'll take it HR and they'll fire his ass."

I had an idea. *I* would surreptitiously record that meeting — the baiting session. There, Terry set the first bait, "Gays are all the same — They love tapestries." I said nothing. Then Lee the other supervisee set the sexism bait: "You know, girls just want to have fun." I didn't react. Then Terry moved to the racism bait: "We're having such trouble with our Black employees." Again, I refused to rise to the bait.

I went to the VP of HR and played the clips. Yes, they got fired, but so was I, for not having not told them that their statements were utterly unacceptable.

The Laziest Person

My mother makes me set an alarm clock. I compromised by setting it for 10 AM and then usually click snooze, okay, sometimes three times.

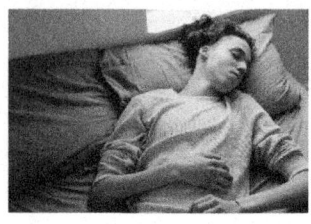

Eren Li, Pexels, CC

Then I crawl out of bed and when I can't get my mother to make me breakfast, I throw a packet of pre-flavored oatmeal into a paper cup (so I don't have to wash a dish) add water, toss it in the microwave, and I'm done.

My mother has made me take a job: licking envelopes — There actually is a job licking envelopes. Of course, I line up five envelopes at a time and run a sponge over them all.

Then, if my mother is out, I take a nap, watch a sitcom, or do some weed, sometimes all three. If she's there, I pretend to be applying for jobs but I never click "Send."

Then one day, my father, who I had never seen, shows up at the door. He came to visit my mother and me after all these years. And he gave me hell: "You lazy piece of shit. You don't deserve the air you breathe. You should be ashamed of yourself, you useless turd!"

I just shrugged and he stormed off to talk with my mother. But somehow, and I'm embarrassed to admit it, that, of all things, worked. I made myself set the alarm for 9:00 with a maximum of one push of the snooze button and actually clicked "Send" on a few jobs.

I'd be lying to you to say that now all's good but maybe I'm giving myself a chance.

Power Imbalance

I was pleased to have been hired in Dr. Lee's lab as a research scientist. After all, Silicon Valley Institute of Technology is among the world's premier universities for basic science research and Dr. Lee is preeminent in the area of single-cell proteomics.

Nick Youngson CC BY-SA 3.0
Pix4free.org

A couple weeks after I began, I attended the required sexual harassment training. Everyone in the lab was there and it was led by a person from HR. She was very clear, perhaps even tough, about reporting even a potential case of sexual harassment.

Over the coming months, Dr. Lee, pleased with my work and, I suppose, liking me as a person, maybe even as a woman, spent more time mentoring me. The HR person occasionally came to our lab for various reasons and it seemed that she looked just an extra moment when Dr. Lee and I interacted.

The last time was when Dr. Lee had come to my workstation and, while leaning over to see what was on my screen, he rested his hand on my shoulder. The HR person happened to walk by, saw it, and perhaps intuiting she would disapprove, he pulled his hand away a bit quickly, which she may have interpreted as guilt. She asked me to step away — "I need to talk to you."

She walked me down the hall and into an empty office and said, "I'll come to the point. I have made abundantly clear that a case of even potential harassment should be reported to me. That's especially the case when there is a power imbalance, and doubly so when the perpetrator is your boss. Both are operative here.

"Perpetrator?" I blurted. He hasn't done anything.

"You're young. You're naive."

I'm not proud of what I did but it felt instinctive, automatic, like a knee reflex. I went from 0 to 60 in one second and I shoved her.

She stepped back and said, "I see." She nodded in a way that suggested she would "write me up."

I stormed out and asked Dr. Lee if, after work, he'd like to go out for a drink. He smiled and said, "I'd like that."

In Tune

I'm 84 years old and thinking about moving to a senior community to take pressure off my daughter, who looks in on me all the time.

With permission, 18/1 Graphics Studio

Work Stories

Before I go, I've long had a desire to play a little piano concert, not at some fancy place, just in my living room on the little spinet piano that I've used more for decoration than for playing. All I can play are ridiculously old songs like Moonlight Bay, Over There, and Let Me Call You Sweetheart.

I practiced for a few months and then placed a little ad for my concert in my neighborhood's newsletter.

Then I realized that I hadn't had the piano tuned, ever. So I went to the local piano shop and on the bulletin board, there were business cards for a bunch of piano technicians. Only one was a woman and so—let me be honest with you—Even at my age, I like women—so I called her. I was surprised that she was able to come, same day.

I soon found out why. She had just printed up the business cards and I would be her first customer. I figured that for a duffer like me and a piano that's probably worth less than a tuning costs, she'd be fine. Certainly, my piano could be her guinea pig.

Because she said I'd be her first customer, I figured she was young. But when she walked in the door, she was around my age!

She tuned the piano fine although I'm sure I couldn't tell. After she finished, she asked if I wanted to try it out.

Impish me, I played while singing the lyric, "Let me call you sweetheart, I'm in love with you."

She bowed her head. I don't know if was in embarrassment, to reject me, or because she hated my horrible singing voice. But I decided to ask, "Will you come to my concert?" And she nodded.

She was the only person who showed up. I didn't mind and, as it turns out, neither did she.

A Cop in Bed

It's 7 AM and Tommy and Roxanne are still in bed.

Roxanne said, "What's wrong, honey?"

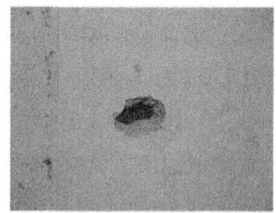

Nichalp, Wikimedia CC 3.0

Tommy said unconvincingly, "I dunno. That can happen even to studs."

Roxanne protested, "But it's been more than a week."

"Maybe the paperwork is getting to me."

Roxanne wasn't convinced: "I know that cops are men of action not of paperwork, but could that explain this?"

"Maybe it's because I'm sad I keep getting passed over for promotion to detective. I know I'm qualified."

"Tommy, I know you. There's something else going on."

With a groan from his bad back, Tommy sat up and looked at his wife of 11 years.

"Roxanne, Internal Affairs is investigating me."

"What did you do?"

"I think I did nothing. It was a domestic. We went in and the guy had a gun pointed down and halfway between his girlfriend and me. I told him to drop it and he didn't and he started to raise it, so I shot the wall to scare him. But now he's claiming that he was dropping the gun. Not true. But what got IAD really going was when— and I swear it's not true— he said that I said, 'Nigger, drop the gun.' I did not!. But his girlfriend is backing him up: "That white cop said, "Drop the fucking gun, nigger!' And then he shot at my boyfriend!" Of course, my partner verified that I was telling the truth. But it's not stopping IAD, and now the media wants to talk with me."

Roxanne said, "Honey it's 7, time to get up."

"Roxanne, I don't have to get up. They've put me on administrative leave. This could cost me my job and I'll never get another one, let alone a promotion. And we're fourth-generation cops. Can you imagine what my father and grandfather will say and worse, what they'll think? And when the media decides it has enough to make it sensational, everyone will see it and I'll lose my friends!"

Roxanne said, "I know you're a good cop but you have said a couple things about African-Americans. Are you sure you weren't being racist?"

Tommy looked at her and cried.

Norma

Norma graduated from Leviathan University with a major in psychology and $132,000 in student debt. Ironically, she took a job in Leviathan's bursar's office as an accounts-receivable clerk.

With permission, 18/1 Graphics Studio

Her job was to send notices to students who were late in paying their student loans and to respond to in-person pleas for forbearance.

It pained Norma to see the endless line of graduates and dropouts who couldn't afford to pay. She thought back to when she was in high school and had been seduced by Leviathan's marketing materials that implied that its graduates are likely to get a well-paying job and explicitly blaring that misleading statistic, "College graduates earn $1 million more."

But Norma had to put such thoughts aside— Her job was to get the alumni and dropouts to pay. So she told student after student, "I'm sorry." And she emailed letter after letter, "Your account is past due. To avoid additional penalties, please remit the balance due within ten days."

But there was a last straw. An alum begged, "I want a job where I can make a difference but I'm saddled with all this not cut out for that. I'm cut out for helping people. I've living with three roommates and still can't afford both my rent and student loan."

On impulse, Norma simply zeroed out the student's account and said, "Your loan is now paid in full. Go make a difference." The student sputtered, "But, but..." Norma waved her away. "Just go."

Within an hour, her boss came in. "Zeus (the computer program) just kicked out a file: Yesterday, this person had a balance of $107,955 and today it's zero?" Norma lied, "I have no idea. Must be a computer glitch."

That bought Norma a little time but she knew that even if she claimed it was a typing error, she'd be out of a job within a day or even go to jail. So she decided to do as much Robin-Hooding as she could in her remaining time.

The next person in line was a guy who came to Leviathan on a football scholarship but after a year, was told there now were better players and he lost his scholarship. He told Norma, "If Leviathan hadn't given me the scholarship, I would have gone to an inexpensive community college. But now, I have a year's worth of credits that may not all transfer and I've made friends here at Leviathan. So I feel stuck. Is there any way you can spread out the payments?" Norma lied again: "I just found a technicality that forgives ex-scholarship athletes' tuition for four years. Congratulations."

At that moment, Norma's boss, who had been hiding within earshot, burst in, along with a cop. "Norma, I can't believe you stole from the university." She retorted, "Every day, the university steals from its students, selling a defective, exorbitant product— I just established a return policy."

Nevertheless, the cop handcuffed Norma and took her away. Norma never felt prouder.

The Toilet Cleaners' Union

The hotel's toilet cleaners agreed to meet in the empty presidential suite.

Amin, Wikimedia, CC 4.0

The Fiery One seethed, "How dare they pay us just $20 an hour and only half our medical benefits. Raise your hand if you'll join me in storming the manager's office!"

She raised her fist and then all the other four did, and they marched into the manager's office. The Fiery One demanded more money and 100% employer-paid health care whereupon the manager for the first time decided to be fully honest with her employees, even if it would cost her job:

> *You are lucky to have your job. You have no skills. 20% of the time, you don't show up, sometimes without even calling in. Yet you get much higher than minimum wage plus I pay 50% of your medical benefits. I make a point of praising you and often give you a free gift card even for a minor thing. I am disappointed in you.*

They retreated back to the presidential suite. "Now what?" a quiet one asked.

Work Stories

The Fiery One roared, "We go on a slowdown! We'll clean those fat cats' toilets just once a week. For once in their life, they can smell their own shit. If they don't like it, they can clean their toilet bowl with toilet paper."

The other four nodded, one vigorously, the others tentatively.

Days passed and not one guest complained, perhaps because toilets don't start to smell so quickly, perhaps because they didn't feel it was worth complaining.

And that was the first example I've heard of quiet quitting.

Big Balls

Vijay Patel looked up at the clock: 6:30 PM. When he first became an engineer, he would have been happy to work for another few hours. But now, he sighed and wished he could quit for the night. Actually, he thought about quitting engineering forever.

With permission, 18/1 Graphics Studio

"But all those years I invested: India Institute of Technology and in climbing the ladder. And what would my friends think? My family? I could hear my grandfather: "What? You're going to open a restaurant. Only the lower castes do that!"

"Actually, I can," he thought. "Indian food is some of the most interesting. And I'd bring my engineer's perfectionism to it. No oily pre-made buffets, in fact nothing pre-made, everything to-order. And, of course, no canned sauces or gulab jamon. Fresh vegetables and I'd buy my spices from my friend Vishnu who imports the best cumin, coriander, clove, cinnamon, turmeric, fenugreek, cardamom, all of it. I'll make the naan right—each piece fresh in the tandoor. To keep prices down, I'll find a location that's good but just dicey enough that the rent will be okay."

And Vijay did all that. And his family ridiculed him. "His mother said, "I am embarrassed. We all are. You're giving up a directorship at Apogee Software to open the ten millionth Indian restaurant? Idiot!"

His son, Subhas, was even more vicious: "You don't know shit about running a restaurant. You'll piss away your savings and go bust within a year. And then no one will hire you—Who'd want a software engineer who quit to open a restaurant and failed, at age 51?"

Vijay did everything he promised himself he would. And discerning customers returned again and again, but there weren't enough of them.

Slowly, Vijay's already marginal business shrank. He felt forced to say yes to the ad salesman who suggested he advertise a 10%-off coupon. That didn't help but Vijay said no to upping it to 25%. "I will not give 25% of what I've worked so hard for!" That's also what he said to the delivery services: Doordash, GrubHub, and UberEats.

But now, Vijay was bleeding serious money and decided to stop minimizing the problem with his son, who was a marketing manager.

Subhas said, "Finally. Thank you, Dad for coming clean. Let me market your business. I can make it successful. The only thing I ask is that you give me three months to do it my way. If you don't like the results, you can go back to your way." Vijay felt he had no choice.

Subhas sprang into action. He decided that the key would be to make the restaurant cool to Gen Z'ers. Vijay's Indian Restaurant? Stodgy. Mumbai Mambo? Better but mambo is for old people. Ah, we'll make the gulab jamon (round dessert balls) huge and call the restaurant, Big Balls.

Decor? We can save: cheap posters of Gen-Z performers. And we can name dishes and drinks after them, like Beyonce Biryani and the Taylor Swift cocktail— It gets you drunk swiftly.

We'll bring in live music. I know I can convince Gen-Z bands to do it for exposure to their target market, plus it's a date magnet.

Servers? I'll visit a few malls and hire away good cellphone salespeople, offering them commission on appetizers, drinks, high-priced entrees, and desserts. To help them and myself, I'll have tabletop tents for appetizers, drinks, and desserts.

Our plates are stupid. Yeah, they're hand-painted from India but the rims are narrow. That means you gotta put more food on the plate to make it look full enough. I'll steal a lesson from frou-frou restaurants: ultra-wide-rim plates and in white, so the contrast with the food's color makes it look like there's more food on the plate.

And no more free naan. And I'll charge a lot for it— I don't want them filling up on bread. I want them to pay for big-ticket, high-margin stuff: drinks, appetizers, entrees, and dessert.

To further discourage naan while saving money, no more making it fresh in the tandoor—storebought and thrown in the microwave.

It took too long for dad to make the dishes to order, so I'll use canned sauces. They're not bad. I'll have the cook put them in black plastic bags—In the dumpster in back of a frou-frou Italian restaurant, I once saw a bunch of empty cans of canned sauce. I don't want my customers to see that I use canned.

But using canned sauce, I need to get dad out of the kitchen—He'd be furious. Maybe I can do it if I flatter him into saying he'd be a great maitre'd. Nope. Wrong demographic—I'll use hot college girls. I gotta get him to work the back office—He said he'd give me three months to do it my way.

Okay, onto publicity. I'll make funny videos on TikTok and Insta, like holding up two Big Balls. Also, organic is hot so I'll say, "We love organic." That doesn't mean it needs to be 100% organic. Maybe just some organic spices would do.

I'm not allowed to solicit Yelp or Google reviews but I can get around that. I'll tell the servers that whenever a customer praises the restaurant, to give a card I'll print up. One side will have a GenZ-oriented riddle like, "When does 1+1 = 3? When you don't use a condom."

On the back, the card will say, "We're loved on Yelp and Google." That'll get the point across without our soliciting reviews.

I'll need media reviews, so I'll research all the main restaurant reviewers and find their hot button. For example, if I see one who also reviews weed, I'll send 'em a joint of primo stuff— Not so much that it seems like a bribe but enough to make them laugh, feel good about me, and come review the restaurant.

I *am* going to use Doordash, Grubhub, and UberEats. I'll hire some kid to go to nearby office buildings, go to each office and offer to leave takeout menus with the receptionist.

I'll start with moderate prices but raise them as soon as I can. Not only does the public foolishly assume that higher price means better food, the bigger profit will get me a higher price when I sell the business, which I will as soon as business starts to level off.

Vijay fought the bowdlerizing of his ethically crafted restaurant, but Subhas kept reminding him of their deal: three months.

It didn't happen within three months but six months later, Subhas got his father to agree to sell Big Balls to Restaurant Holdings Group which promised, "We'll have the restaurant honor Vijay's legacy while maintaining Subhas' modern approach." But a year later, Restaurant Holdings Group gutted Vijay's restaurant to the studs and replaced it with the newest hot restaurant concept.

Burn

I always had a short fuse. My father nicknamed me, "Burn." My parents are the opposite: quiet, calm.

LAPD, CC2.0

I not only loved but respected my parents, in part because I wish I had their personality.

That love and respect, plus my liking living with them, and, to be honest, being a little scared to go to an away-college, made me wonder if I should just go to the local commuter college. But I did go away, in part because I was curious about the "lifetime friendships" that the colleges' marketing touted.

But my experience in the dorm made that unlikely. I couldn't stand all the silliness: partying hard in the middle of the week, many kids drunk or stoned a fair amount in between, and tradezee sex: That was the kids' term for everyone screwing everyone. I found it all lazy and— a fancy word I learned in college: dissolute. Actually, I felt angry about it all— at them, at the colleges' marketing BS, and even at myself for not fitting in.

At Christmas, I told my parents that I was thinking of transferring to a commuter college. They urged me to give it another try. I agreed but insisted that they let me live in an apartment. They agreed as long as I took a part-time job to help pay for it.

During the Christmas holiday, more than they ever had, my parents went into detail about why my mother left the house in the middle of the night twice—The cops had called to say her store had been arsoned. The cops said that the community doesn't like Asian businesses in their neighborhood. Then, my dad talked about what it was really like for his grandparents in the Japanese internment camps in World War II.

To try to understand it all, including my own reactions and my own personality, I majored in psychology and, while I had doubts about the power of the professors' explanation for people's malaise such as family of origin, trauma, and sociological influences, I bought it well enough to stay with the major. And because, afterward, I preferred more school to getting a job, I applied and got into and all the way through a Ph.D. in clinical psychology.

But I found those theories didn't help my clients much. Yes, my clients got more insight into themselves but too rarely was their life much better. As often, the therapy made them feel like victims—They tended to blame their problems mainly on things outside their control. Worse, too many stayed focused on their past rather than on moving forward. I sometimes felt angry at them and at my training.

I knew I needed a new career. I thought about taking my dad's advice and going back for a computer science degree but couldn't make myself do it— I wanted to be my own man. So I tried a variation: I went to a video-game-design bootcamp, but no one would hire me except as a $20-an hour game tester— boring and dead-end.

What have I decided to do? Drive an ice cream truck—at least that's something I believe in and I make every customer happy. Today, my parents threatened to disown me and in anger, on my phone, in front of them, I made a YouTube of me burning my Ph.D. diploma.

Do What You Love?

My most vivid childhood memory was of being in a museum and repulsed that the butterflies were pinned. "How could they stick a dagger into the heart of one of nature's most beautiful animals and then display it for people to gawk at. It's like if my mother stabbed me and hung me on the front lawn."

With permission, 18/1 Graphics Studio

And in high school, the most memorable thing I learned was that in the Western U.S., where I live, over the past four decades, 450 butterfly species have declined at an average of almost two percent a year.

So it was no surprise that when people asked me what I wanted to be when I grew up, I said, "Entomologist, so I can save butterflies."

I was worried that because I was just a B student, I couldn't make it as an entomologist, but I was inspired by the marine biologist who visited my class and urged everyone to "follow your dream!" My favorite TV show was Oprah and many guests echoed that idea: "Dream it and you can do it!" The last line of a video interview of an astronaut was, "Shoot for the moon. Even if you miss, you'll land among the stars."

So in looking for a college, I searched for California colleges that offered an entomology major. There was UC Davis but my grades and test scores were well below its average, but I applied just in case. Then there was UC Riverside, which was a "possible." Alas, I was rejected from both and had to go to my safe school: San Diego State, which didn't offer an entomology major, so I declared a major in biology.

Alas, I struggled with Introduction to Biology for Majors. As inspiration, I chose as my computer's wallpaper, "Do what you love; the money will follow." I joined a study group, asked the professor for help during office hours, and he sent me to the tutoring center. I studied hard, including staying up late the night before tests and, to my relief, I got a B+ in the course.

But in inorganic chemistry, despite even more studying, all the slogans, and all my affirmations that I was a badass, I got only a C+. And I was facing the even harder organic chemistry, physics, and calculus before even being allowed to take Intro to Entomology.

To help remind me why I was doing all this work, I searched the internet to find a summer internship involving butterflies and was happy to learn that the National Butterfly Association sponsors butterfly counts throughout California, including one in "Butterfly Valley," and I signed up.

After an exhausting but rewarding day counting the declining monarch butterflies, my fellow volunteers and I recounted the day and told of our dreams. Could we all make a living as entomologists? After some months or years, will we still feel passionate about butterflies? We disagreed about that but agreed we'd never pin a butterfly.

Driving back home, I had much to think about. Should I follow my passion? If I dream it and work hard, can I actually do it? If I do what I love will the money actually follow? Should I do it even if the money doesn't follow?

A MD and His Starving-Artist Child

Yes, I'm tired, often overwhelmed. You'd think after all those years of pre-med, medical school, internship, residency, and setting up a practice, I'd be entitled to a pretty good life.

Raffael Herrmann, CC0.photo, Public Domain

Yet the Medicare and insurance reimbursements keep getting cut. They think doctors are fat cats to be redistributed from, but when you consider the cost of medical school, malpractice insurance, setting up an office and paying staff, I sometimes wonder if garbage collectors net more.

And all the idealism that fueled my willingness to endure all that has faded. Too many non-compliant, non-paying, or know-it-all patients. Too much paperwork only to often get my request for reimbursement denied or cut. And the stress: I'm making life-and-death decisions all the time and sometimes must give bad news, even fatal news. Plus, it's hard to keep up with what's new. My medical journals are piling up unread—It reminds me of why I canceled my subscription to the New Yorker—I kept feeling guilty that I didn't have time to read them.

Yet when my daughter insisted that she didn't want to be a doctor, not even to go to college, but only to art school, I was sad. Art school—that four-year summer camp that too often leads to the cliche, "starving artist," never making enough even to pay back student loans let alone make a living, even a subsistence living. That's especially so in an era of ever-better AI-created art.

So I decided to tell her that I wouldn't pay for art school but would pay for college as long as her major was even vaguely practical. She enrolled at a local state university, which made sense to me. Despite my moderate net income, I'd still get little financial aid and most of what I did get would be a loan that would have to be paid back with interest. And today, the sticker price of four years at a brand-name coastal private college is $300,000+, and not much less at a brand-name out-of-state public college. And that assumes she graduates in four years. It often takes five or longer and almost half drop out.

When she was home for Christmas, she left her transcript on the kitchen table. It was emblazoned with her major: studio art!

I told her that unless she switched majors, I wouldn't pay. She showed that she is the independent woman I encouraged her to be—She dropped out of college and rather than come back home, lived with three roommates in a dangerous part of the city. She paid for it with a part-time job as a clerk in an art supply store plus government welfare programs: food stamps, housing subsidy, transportation vouchers, some cash aid, even free admission to tourist attractions like museums.

I came to visit her and found her happy, candidly, happier than I am. She said, "I'd rather be a starving artist than an exhausted, burned-out doctor. Dad, are you sure you shouldn't consider a career change?"

I said no but as I was driving home, I started thinking.

53 and Unhirable

Alan was still competent although not quite as sharp, hard-working, or up-to-date as the younger members of the autonomous vehicle team.

He knew he was at risk of getting let go, and he got more concerned when his request to buy a $750 piece of software was rejected. He got even

with permission, 18/1 Graphics Studio

more worried when he was excluded from the monthly meeting with higher-ups.

And then Alan was "laid off"— and terrified. He was his family's primary source of income. He needed another job, and now.

Alan applied to dozens of openings, got three interviews, but no offers: "Overqualified," "Not quite right," and finally, when he was rejected for what he was sure was the perfect job, he phoned the recruiter to ask why. The recruiter was evasive but Alan pushed and the recruiter sighed and said, "You *will* keep this confidential. The bosses said we need more BIPOCs."

After a week of near catatonia and family pressure to bring home the bacon, Alan felt his choices were welfare or retail. As a lifetime tinkerer, he chose a home-improvement chain store at $23 an hour.

Although he hated the 80 percent pay cut, he enjoyed that the other clerks referred difficult customer questions to him.

But working retail soon wore thin and Alan was even revisiting the welfare option when, as he was trudging to the back of the store to take his break, he saw a customer struggling to reach a box of light bulbs from a high shelf.

That reminded him of how often customers had that problem. And Alan spent his break and then the next two months of evenings using his programming and tinkering ability to design a battery-operated mini-lift, much safer and more compact than a ladder. He built a prototype and the chain and other retailers with high shelves were interested—if he could produce them in quantity.

Alan hired other programmers and engineers to design and manufacture *Wanna Lift?* In hiring, he made sure to give fair attention to job candidates of today's 'wrong' demographics.

After just a year, Alan and the other three founders never again had to worry about being discriminated against.

No Fuckin' Way

A bunch of us were getting out of prison soon. I picked three guys who seemed smart, reliable, and not crazy.

During exercise time, we were huddling and, of course, the guard barked, "What's going on here?" I explained that we're planning to start a security business when we get out—It's hard for felons to find a job, so we figured we'd start our own business. We'd call it, No Fuckin' Way.

pxfuel, free to use

We did it in the worst neighborhoods. All kinds of stores hired us: nightclubs, jewelry stores, shoe stores, all kinds of stores. And we stopped a bunch of robberies, even an assault—After all, we're not exactly new to this kind of thing.

But the police shut us down—"Vigilantism is against the law." The other two guys are already back in the joint but I decided to apply to the police academy to become a cop. I said that my background would actually make me a good candidate. I applied to ten and one accepted me.

Today is the day I graduated from the Academy and I am going to be a cop. My two partners in No Fuckin' Way gave me a standing O—It was the best moment of my life.

I Can't Even Give Away My Books

A sane person would have given up by now.

My first book was light-years from a bestseller: It sold 17 copies, and 14 were to my family and friends. My new one has sold a grand total of six, count 'em six. Even my family quickly got sick of buying my books.

Matt Zhang, Flickr, CC 2.0

And it's not that I haven't tried to sell them. After all, they say that after you've crossed the last t and dotted the last i, you're only half done. The rest is marketing and unless you're Oprah, it's all on you. So every day, I flog.

Of course, I post on social media, and not just announcing the book — a million are published each year. No — I give away excerpts of my fiction book, *Tom's Tale* and a Tip of the Week from my how-to book, *Bossing Your Boss.)* I run contests, even offering a free book for the first three people to say why they like or hate it. (Not one response.)

I post on Twitter, LinkedIn, and Facebook. My friends say, "But what about TikTok and Instagram?" I visited — We all must have *some* standards.

I ask to speak at libraries, bookstores, service clubs, MeetUps, and churches — Usually crickets, and the few times I spoke, I had optimistically brought ten books but sold just one or two. I visited my local college campus at noon and offered the books free to passersby. Almost no one has taken one — I can't even give away my books.

I even donated ten to the local mental hospital — A friend had told me they like to give books to patients, but only softcovers. They're too likely to use a hardcover as a weapon.

I hate to admit it but despite it all, I'm starting to write book three: *Tales of an Utterly Unsuccessful Author.* Think it'll sell?

Work Stories

Grandpa's Beg

Just before grandpa died, his family around the bed, he whispered his last words: "Live simpler." No one said anything…and for good reason.

JL Field, PublicDomainPictures

You see, the Girard family liked their far-from-simple life. Despite the San Francisco Bay Area's traffic, crime, and taxes, they liked their mini-manse, Lexi, and five-star vacations.

But then Mr. Girard lost his job as a private-equity valuator—Bye-bye 700K salary. And because of what he was sure was a "demographic reason," he couldn't find another job despite Mrs. Girard flogging him after he had become dispirited and couldn't make himself write yet another customized BS-rich version of his resume.

Then the bank came calling — Bay Area mini-manses don't come cheap and the meter runs 24/7/365. The Girards forestalled by canceling the country club and gym memberships and their gardener and housecleaner. But as the months rolled on, savings from the spending-centric Girards dwindled as the bank's dunning letters got meaner.

Their home now in pre-foreclosure, they were no longer able to brush off grandpa's dying words.

So they sold their house and moved to a small one just outside the town of Spring Valley, Idaho. Even though it came with a half-acre, it cost 80% less than they got for their Bay Area house. That gave the Girards a good few years to figure out how to make money.

But it didn't take that long. They were surprised to find that the town didn't have a cafe, nor a bookstore. So they opened a bookstore cafe.

Another surprise, because of Idaho's cold climate, the fruit was crappy. So their son, the precocious Andy, 12, Googled to learn how to grow great tomatoes in a cool-summer climate. Of course, you need to pick the right varieties, like the taste-test-winning cherry tomato *Orange Paruche,* but there are tricks to add heat. For example, plant the tomatoes along a fence that you paint with white, heat-reflecting paint: That raised the temperature around the tomatoes five, sometimes ten, degrees. On weekends and after school, Andy sat at a table in front of the cafe selling the tomatoes to the amazed customers.

Speaking of school, Andy liked Spring Valley School better than school in the Bay Area because the work wasn't "so Woke" and the kids weren't competing on such silliness as who had designer-label ripped jeans.

Mrs. Girard started a book club that met weekly at the bookstore cafe and then a writer's group, both of which generated book sales, Amazon be damned.

Mr. Girard was happier running his bookstore cafe than gutting businesses, which too often was done in the private-equity business.

And if there's a heaven, grandpa is smiling.

Work Stories

The Barkery and Me

I guess I should first tell you that I'm a dog. I'm not yappy, nor happy, I'm just energetic, although my owner — actually I prefer "caretaker" — jokes that I should go on Ritalin — intravenously.

My dog, Hachi. Photo credit: own work

I don't want to tell you about my, okay, owner. He's fine but ordinary — always remembers to feed, walk, and yes pet me. And of course, I sleep in his bed. Dog beds, let alone crates? Never, ever.

He got me a job where he works: The Barkery — It makes dog biscuits. Yeah, they're healthy but we sell them to supermarkets where they don't cost an arm and a paw, unlike at frou-frou doggie boutiques, let alone dog spas. Dog spas?! Gimme a break, or a bark.

My job is VP of Comfort. I go from desk to desk, looking up at the person, hoping for a pet. No response? I raise my paw. Still no go, I move on. Of course, sometimes the person also gives me a Doggie Delight cookie, but not that often (sigh) —I guess they don't want me to get fat.

What I want to tell you about is yesterday, Christmas Eve. Of course, we all got to home early. We closed at noon, amazing, noon! But at 11:45, I got the most amazing Christmas present. The president of the company called us all in and said, "I'd like to introduce a new employee who I know will fit right in." There was a box wrapped in Christmas paper but it must have been defective because it had lots of holes in it. He opened it and there was my dream come true — another cockapoo! He said, "This is Renee."

Immediately, Renee trotted to me, sniffed my genitals to be sure I was okay, then lifted her paw to signal that she wanted to play. I sure did. Renee is the best Christmas present I've ever gotten.

A Salesman Turned Fundraiser Talks to His Dog

I shouldn't have chosen a career as a salesman and now, its nonprofit equivalent: fundraiser. I was seduced by the "infinite income potential," which turns out to be, at best, an overstatement. Too often, if you do too well, they cap your income, lower your commission rate, change your territory, some shit like that. Worse, selling, including nonprofit fundraising, is very stressful — Make your number or you get a worse prospect list, or even worse, you're out.

Antoni Shkraba, Pexels, CC

So when day is done, I need to process it all, and my favorite listener is my dog, Gretchen. Here's a paraphrase of what I said to her today. Admittedly it was a particularly bad day at work.

Gretchen, I thought I'd be happier pitching the museum than Dodge cars. But it's as, well, dodgy. I can't help but worry about asking people to donate to an art museum.

Yes, they're rich and yes, some of them got their money by stretching the truth, but so do I. And most of those people work hard for their money. Can I really look them in the eye and say that donating to an art museum or to a university that has plenty of money and too often Wokeizes its students are the best uses of their charity dollars when deep down I believe that, for example, cancer, Planned Parenthood, and Goodwill are better causes? I tried to get a job selling for a better cause than the art museum but competition for those is crazy.

Maybe it's time to cut my losses and throw a party for all the people who like me and ask them if they know of someone who could hire me for something different — I have no idea what that would be.

In the meantime, I'm going to take you for a walk, dear Gretchen. You can pee and I can de-stress.

A Dancer Talks to Her Dog

I do ballet, and we all have to act like dance is everything. No one would dare express doubts. I'm not going to stick my neck out.

Pixabay, CC

So today, I decided to spill my guts to my dog, Arabesque. Here's the essence of what I said.

I've put in all this time to learn ballet and, when I'm on stage, it's fun but it's getting to be less fun. And I'm on stage only a few minutes for every ten hours I'm rehearsing or practicing on my own.

And my feet are starting to get bad — No surprise. That's happening to all of us.

So Arabesque, I'm just about ready to quit. But to what? Teach dance? I'd still have to live with my parents. Something outside of dance? I have no idea what. I'm not going to be a computer programmer or a carpenter or a salesperson.

Arabesque, did I make a mistake putting all this time and effort into ballet? I can't think about it now. Arabesque, do you want to go for a walk, or watch me practice for my next performance?

A Musician Talks to His Dog

Part of why I became a musician is because I'm an introvert, not social. I'm more comfortable playing. So when I want to talk, especially about something important, I talk, would you believe, to my dog, Billy. Here's a paraphrase of what I just said to him:

The author. Photo credit: Dianne Woods

Yeah, I like being a musician but even though I'm a busy professional, I'm barely scraping by. Only the famous make real money. Is it time for me to grow up and get a straight job? Nah, I'm not ready for that yet.

I need to work on something:

My playing? I guess, but I'm pretty good.

My image? I probably need to be edgier — maybe a purple streak in my hair, maybe gyrate more at the keyboard, I dunno.

I probably should market myself more. Like send bigger bands some links to my SoundCloud and YouTubes. I've told myself to do that a lot of times, but I really should. I think this time, I will.

Hey, Billy, what do you think? Yeah, I know what you think. You think I should give you a treat. I already gave you two today but what the heck?

Warrior and "Wimp"

I can't understand how any of us could be against unionizing. I mean, we'd get job security — They couldn't just let us go whenever they please. If they treat a worker badly, let alone are racist, sexist, or homophobic, the union would defend her or him. Most important, we'd have the power of the collective to negotiate for more money, more benefits, more everything!

Courtesy, TJUnion

Yet Mandy is thinking about voting no. At a meeting, she said something like, "They treat us well. If we unionize, it'll be more contentious. And if everyone gets the same pay and can't get fired, we'll have no motivation. The customers will suffer. And just look at

Safeway's employees — They're unionized and always look sad. Do you want Trader Joe's to become like that?"

She just doesn't get it. What a wimp!

Well today, of all people, Mandy, who was on break, came to my line, handed me one of our bouquets. I was polite and said, "Mandy, I can't accept this." She walked away and a minute later returned with one of our chocolate hearts. This time, I was more direct: "Amanda, no." She walked away and returned with a jar of sour pickles. I couldn't restrain myself from laughing and, having softened me up, she asked, "Wanna take a walk after work?" I said yes.

Puff Piece

I didn't fit in. In class, I did badly because I was dyslexic. Outside of class, I was awkward. I didn't know how to make conversation and felt hurt when kids made me the butt of a joke. I didn't realize that the right thing to do is to laugh it off or even to dish some back, playfully, so they don't think you're actually angry. I wish I knew that then.

Kolforn, Wikimedia, Free for use

So I kind of avoided kids. At recess, I'd stay in classrooms to help the teachers, but really, it was to help myself, to avoid feeling awkward with the other kids.

Work Stories

After school, I worked at an artisan cheese shop. I was just walking by it one day on the way home from school and saw a part-time help-wanted sign. I guess it isn't easy to get someone, so even though I was just 17 and had no work experience, let alone with cheese—I ate Velveeta!—the owner hired me. My job was just to clean up and slice and wrap cheese.

Cheesemakers would often come in to try to get the owner to sell their cheeses. One day, a brie maker came in. I asked him how it's made. I guess he was impressed that I'd ask, so he asked if I wanted to work a couple hours each night turning the brie and Camembert rounds—You see, they need to be turned every eight hours, and because his operation was small, he couldn't afford "Tina the Turner," the $50,000 cheese-turning machine.

I grew to love his cheeses and that job—I was well-suited to the repetitive, solo work. I didn't have to worry that I was dyslexic, I didn't have to be social, and it gave me time to think. Somehow, one night, I thought about other French delicious things, and croissants popped to mind. What if our cheeses could be wrapped in croissant dough?

I told the owner who was intrigued. He researched it, figured out how it could be done and, long story short, he first made it in small quantities and when it sold out quickly in cheese shops, he sold the recipe and process to a larger cheese company.

He split the money 50/50 with me and asked if I want to be his partner. Of course, I said yes and now I'm thinking about how our croissant-wrapped cheese might otherwise be used—My current idea: selling it to French restaurants to crown their French onion soup. We'll see.

Astronaut or Homemaker?

When I was a little girl, I read a book about Christa McAuliffe, the female astronaut who died. I thought, "I want to be an astronaut. I won't die."

JRico144, Pixabay, Free to use

But unlike many kids with, ahem, flights of fancy, I stayed with it. And it turned out to be not quite as hard as the book said. I joined the Air Force, got picked to fly jets, got my 1,000 pilot-in-command hours, and the required master's degree, and passed NASA's week-long long-duration flight physical. I was surprised at what I found hardest: They test your hand and eye coordination after having been in virtual space for a week—Everything felt distorted.

Then I had two interviews at the Johnson Space Center—questions I wouldn't have expected—about my family, aerospace innovations I liked, and a time I had to keep a secret—Astronauts have to keep a lot confidential.

Then there was a year of astronaut training, much in the weightless simulator. That's not as fun as they portray in the movies. Yes, it's fun to float around but you also, for example, have to move heavy objects. You might think that's easy, but because there's no friction, those objects can easily float away. One time, a heavy box did. I raced—as fast as you can when floating—but couldn't catch it and it banged into the instrumental panel. But as always, my instructors were forgiving.

Fast forward and I was in the cockpit of the spaceship Levitate on a mission to Mars. The first manned mission to Mars—just a fly-by—was in 2033, when the Earth-to-Mars distance was minimum, requiring only a 570-day trip. My trip was longer, not just because of the greater distance but because it was the first to land on Mars.

When I heard the famous, "3, 2, 1, liftoff!" and we indeed lifted off, I was nervous, exhilarated but nervous—I did think of Christa McAuliffe.

And would you believe, at 66,000 feet, we sprang a leak and started to lose altitude, but we fixed it. Nonetheless, I remained vigilant, okay nervous, the entire flight.

640 days, including five on Mars collecting soil (mainly red dust), rock, air, and water samples, and then we returned to Earth without a hitch.

Now I have a daughter and love telling her my astronaut stories. Guess what she wants to do as a career? Be a homemaker. I would have preferred and been flattered if she wanted to be an astronaut, but to be honest, I can understand.

A Coffee Tree Grows in Brooklyn

I thought, "Who the hell could be calling me at 3 in the morning?"

It was the police: "A thief, working 'graveyard shift', broke your store's window. You need to come and turn off the alarm."

I raced to my store, Cawfee Tawk, and went limp: Three 50-pound bags of coffee, my so-carefully selected best beans in the world, stolen!

Coffee tree, Ekrem Canli, Wikimedia, CC 4.0

I thought, maybe it's a blessing. I needed a final push to take a break. The crime, the noise, the traffic, customers running out without paying, cars outside blasting music over the soft music I play in the cafe to create an island of sanity in crazy Brooklyn.

Where should I go? Trying to be practical, I thought about visiting a supplier—It would be tax-deductible. Ethiopia? It's one of the world's poorest countries, nah. Peru? Near the equator, nope. Hawaii! This guy, Kai, has a tiny farm in an area I had never heard of Ka'u.

I called Kai and asked how he'd feel about a visitor. He couldn't have shown more, well, aloha. So, off I went. And even the baby two rows away crying nonstop, especially on landing, didn't dampen my excitement.

From Hilo Airport, it was a 90-minute drive along the coast, passing not just waves rolling onto black-sand beach, but volcanoes and tropical plants. It definitely wasn't Brooklyn, and I was glad.

When I arrived at Kai's Ka'u Coffee Farm, it was smaller even than I expected, maybe the size of a football field.

Kai must have heard my car pull up, because with his mane of long, black hair—in contrast with my bald brown fringe—he strode from the coffee field to greet me—Aloha continued.

It was hard to know what to say, so after I said aloha—That must have sounded patronizing, cultural appropriation, or just plain stupid—I just smiled and handed him the care package I had brought—Brooklyn goodies that go with coffee: cheese danish, chocolate babka, and ruggelach: croissant dough with chocolate chips.

Kai invited me into his cafe next to the farm and we bonded quickly.

He said—and he seemed sincere—that he loved all three of my pastries, especially the ruggelach. And I gushed truthfully, that his coffee—with a weird name—Bourbon Yellow—was the best I had ever tasted.

I told him what happened to my store and about Brooklyn's crime and noise. He explained that he used to work in downtown Honolulu but the crime and noise got to him too—far from the idyllic marketing PR. More bonding.

Kai had long wanted to be a farmer, learned that the Ka'u district had perfect soil for coffee but was little-known, so he could afford a small plot.

Another bond was unexpected—He said he was getting a little bored with farming. That helped me realize that after ten years running Cawfee Tawk, I was kind of bored too. So we agreed to trade places for a month. He taught me what I needed to know and I taught him what he needed.

No, it didn't work out perfectly. I had to be on Zoom with him nearly daily to keep the coffee trees from dying, and he had to be on Zoom with me to learn how to pay bills, make better cappuccino, and yes, deal with difficult customers.

After the month, Kai returned to his farm and I frankly was relieved. I'm better suited to a cafe in Brooklyn than a coffee farm in Ka'u. And Kai said he missed the quiet of his farm, but has now decided to hire help.

As we said goodbye, he asked if I'd sell him shipments of ruggelach for his cafe. I said, "As long as you keep selling me Yellow Bourbon." He smiled and said, "And I'd like to give you this sapling of Yellow Bourbon. When you get home, put it in a good-sized pot in a warm spot, and when winter comes, put it inside in a sunny window over a tray of pebbles to keep the humidity up, and I'll bet you can grow your own. We laughed at that double entendre, hugged, and said good-bye.

It's been a year and I can confirm that, indeed, a coffee tree can grow in Brooklyn.

A Seven-Fingered Pianist

This story is true, well, mainly true.

It was quite a way to get famous, but I'm getting ahead of myself.

The author at the piano. Courtesy, Dianne Woods

I grew up in a tenement in the Bronx. When I was four, my mother was walking me around the block when we came to a vacant lot. There sat a rickety piano—no doubt rained on, snowed on. But that didn't matter to kids—they were happily banging on it. Then one kid started to play what I later learned was Chopsticks, and I was fascinated. I watched and, more important, I listened. When the kids left, I pulled my mother to the piano and, trial and error, mostly error, I tried to plunk out Chopsticks.

Fast forward to when I was 13. I got my first paying gig—New Year's Eve at an Air Force base. Then it was at a Bronx bar—Picture a callow 13-year-old leading a bunch of drunks in When Irish Eyes are Smiling. Then I played in a band that played at wedding and bar-mitzvah receptions.

I was just one of a zillion work-a-day keyboard players.

Ironically, it was a setback, a big one, that made me famous. I developed a rare disease that rendered three of my fingers pretty useless.

Here's the fictional part:

A friend of mine was a journalist and, capitalizing on the societal trend that venerates have-nots, wrote a piece called, "The Seven-Fingered Pianist." He was right: Social media and then CNN and the New York Times picked it up. But what really catapulted me was when I appeared on the Oprah Show.

Now I get to give concerts all over the country, and upcoming: a world tour. Who would have thought that a pianist losing three fingers would be the key to success? Maybe I should cut off a couple more fingers.

Back to the truth: Here is a YouTube of me playing the piano https://tinyurl.com/367kr9uk with, yes, just seven fingers.

BeautEase Roses

My grandfather taught me how to hybridize roses. That was 50 years ago and it's been my obsession ever since. My goal: rose bushes small enough for the typical rose gardener, a retiree, to grow. It must be covered with flowers all season like a geranium but with perfect rose form and be so disease-resistant that it needn't be sprayed.

This is a yet unnamed rose hybridized by the author that's under test for commercial introduction.
Photo credit: Marty Nemko, Free to reuse

Over the 50 years, I have made thousands of crosses, evaluated each, and slowly have developed better and better rose bushes. And after said 50 years, I had developed a line of what I called *BeautEase roses*: a velvety red that I named *I Love You*, a two-tone pink *First Blush*, a bright yellow *Sunny Days*, and a pure white, *Pure*.

A multinational corporation bought the exclusive rights to *BeautEase* roses. I was surprised at the offer's generosity, especially because selling rose bushes seemed a new business for them. Yes, they imported cut rose blossoms from Colombia but this was different. The corporation had many divisions, selling hundreds of products, so I figured they must know what they're doing.

I kept asking them when they'd introduce my roses and they said, "Soon." and they eventually stopped answering my emails. That got me nervous, so I did what I should have done upfront—investigated the company more carefully. It turns out that their most profitable products are the raw ingredients that go into rose fungicides. Because my BeautEase roses were both spectacular and not requiring spraying, if sales took off, it would cut deeply into their business. More investigation made clear that they paid me so the roses *wouldn't* get introduced.

I sued and they settled by returning the rights to my roses plus $50,000, chump change for them. I used the money to hire a salesperson who sells BeautEase roses to nurseries, from mom-and-pops to big-box stores. Now, BeautEase roses are, as they say, available at fine stores near you.

Just When You Feel Safest

Jen was the smartest one in the room. At most staff meetings, she had the best ideas, often topping others'. The unfortunate— as you'll see—very unfortunate side effect is that she made others feel less-than, a no-no in today's workplace.

With permission, 18/1 Graphics Design Studio

So when a "restructuring" resulted in three of the team losing their job, they couldn't help but think that Jen's "showing off" contributed.

One day, Jen was at her desk, the place she felt most comfortable, and a plastic bomb that had been placed under her keyboard exploded, giving her first-degree burns on her hands. Wrapped in aluminum foil was a note, "Remember Psycho? *She* felt safest in her shower until there, she was stabbed to death. Restructure yourself out of a job or else."

The police took the usual report and investigated, of course, interviewing the three laid-off workers, but all had solid alibis—One of them had hired one of the janitors to do the dirty work. In a week, the case joined the 95% that end up in the cold-case file.

Two months passed and Jen, having refused to quit her good job, was relaxed driving home. She had long felt her car was what she called, "My island of sanity." The peace was broken when a bomb that had been placed in the seat-back pocket exploded, burning and wrenching her back. A foil-wrapped note said, "Quit your job or else" and the investigation turned up nothing.

A year later, in the shower, the shower head exploded, bloodying her face.

This time, Jen quit but despite being the smartest one in the room, she couldn't land a decent job. During the interviews, she'd be asked "Why'd you leave your previous job?" She wanted to answer honestly and the interviewer's response inevitably would be something like, "Well, won't this person keep doing it to you again?"

And Jen remained unemployed for a year and scared for life.

"Workers of the World, Unite!"

Kevis, Deviant Art, CC

I can't say I was *happy* at work but it was okay. But when a union organizer came to our store to try to get us to unionize — "Workers of the World, Unite!" — some of our more outspoken employers cheered, including my best friend at work.

For the next month, employees campaigned pro and con, and my friend urged me to vote yes. The day before the vote, the union's community organizer held a rally and party. We got the fervor, I voted yes, and the vote went 23 yes, 18 no. So now we are unionized.

Of course, we are all happy about the additional security of employment and the strength in numbers that let us negotiate with more power.

But the day to day hasn't been as clearly positive. The union rep quietly told us that faster workers should *not* shouldn't work more than the minimum. She said something like, "If we work more than the minimum, fewer people will get hired and more laid off. Besides, do we really want to fill the pockets of the owners and shareholders?"

Another thing. On one hand, it feels good that everyone gets the same pay, but on the other hand, it feels wrong that better workers aren't paid more. I know that for me and I'm guessing others, that's another reason I won't do more than the minimum.

One more thing. The union rep urged us that we felt aggrieved, to file a grievance with the union.

So, no surprise, the managers have become more careful about what they ask us to do. They're even joking less.

Before, a number of customers told me that they choose our supermarket in part because it felt good. But one customer, a regular, just told me that she feels the vibe has gotten worse. When I asked her what she meant, she said something like, "The employees seem a little more serious and when, before, clerks would automatically bag my groceries, now, I occasionally get a look that implies, "So, you won't bag them yourself?" I'm wondering if we'll lose customers.

I love the security, the power, and that the job is easier, but we're all a little more tense and contentious. Was voting to unionize the right decision? Maybe it's too early to tell.

Feedback

The usual response was no response. I felt lucky even to get a form-letter rejection—"There were so many excellent submissions..."

So I tried submitting to outlets that promised feedback—for a fee. I also joined a writer's group. I even spent the $1,995 on a writer's workshop.

With permission, 18/1 Graphic Studio

I got feedback but wasn't confident it would levitate me over the golden threshold into The Land of the Published. Some of the feedback felt too global, for example, "Your chapters are episodic." "Episodic" is insider-speak for chapters that are insufficiently meshed. Or the feedback felt too granular: "I wish Doreen's rationale for choosing Tuskegee was fleshed out."

Mostly, I didn't agree with the feedback. Worse, I felt that if I incorporated much of it, the work wouldn't be me anymore. It would be me hollowed-out or dressed incongruously.

Yes, I adopted a few of the suggestions, for example, replacing some adjectives with verbs, balancing action with breathing space, and eliminating extra words so the resulting soup was distilled. But basically, I decided, the hell with them.

So I self-published my novel, *Before*. I enjoyed having control over not just its words but its formatting and especially its cover: an impressionist hourglass with purple sand. I appreciated that it was available on Amazon one day after I submitted the manuscript.

I've sold a grand total of 37 copies, actually six copies— I bought the other 31 to give as presents. But I've started on the sequel, *During*, and then hope to write *After*.

A Lazy Career Coach

In fetal position with Sigmund under his arm, David finally rejoined the living. The alarm clock said 10:07 AM. "That's okay. I have only one client and she's not until 2," he said to Sigmund in morning-voice."

With permission 18/1 Graphic Studio

David stretched— that pleasant introduction to the day. He rested Sigmund on his pillow and thought, "How can they make a plush dog so soft?"

David twisted out of bed, took off his shorts so the scale wouldn't overweigh him by those few ounces: 175. "Okay, I can have French toast."

Old people tend to value routine but at just 32, so did David. So he kept his "Coulda Been a Contender" t-shirt not hung-up but on the chair next to his bed for easy access. He also enjoyed shuffling to the kitchen. "It's a freedom that old people have: to worry less about their appearance." Then it was his coffee-making ritual: He opened the oxygen-expelling canister to reveal the fair-traded, whole-bean, mocha java. While it was grinding, he put the filter into the Mr. Coffee plus his secret weapon: cinnamon.

Soon, David was back in bed with coffee, Sigmund, and the newspaper. But guilt seeped in and David reached for his copy of the 2024 edition of The Friendly Career Guide— the annually revised 10-million-sold king of career-advice books. "Sigmund, that book is so generous, so folksy, so caring, with anecdote after anecdote, from workplaces, colleges, factories, unemployment lines. Just listen to this one from a prison:

> I believed Jim when he said he'd never murder again. I put my hand on his shoulder and said, 'Let's figure this out.' I asked not just about his skills and interests but about his hopes and dreams. Even murderers have them, and my job was to resurrect them and him."

David couldn't make himself keep reading. It reminded him that he could be doing more for his career coaching clients. Why am I lazy? Is it despite or because grandpa said, "Look at ze numbers on my arm and I'm still here. Vy? Voik: Me and 38 men dug a tunnel out of the kemp, the fucking kemp. Voik, David, voik. Dun be lazy."

I don't think I'm rebelling against him. That's not why I'm lazy, but who knows?

To fool himself that he was still reading, David just flipped through the book and, at the end, noticed "Recommended Career Coaches." He thought, "I wouldn't put me on that list."

At the end of the aforementioned 2:00 session, David asked, "So, would you like to make another appointment? The client replied, "'I'll get back to you." David thought, "I need the money but don't like being salesy." So he just said, "I understand."

After the client clicked off the Zoom, David turned to Sigmund: "I'll never see that client again. Some say, 'I'll get back to you.' Others ghost you. Still others say, 'I just can't afford more sessions right now.' What they really mean is, "You're not worth the money or the time.' And they're right. I became a career coach mainly because I wanted to show grandpa that I valued work without my having to work hard."

David couldn't think about that anymore and distracted himself with, "I have no more clients today so maybe I can take a nap." And he took Sigmund back to bed. But seeing the bed reminded him of his laziness.

He couldn't make himself read more of The Friendly Career Guide, so he compromised by deciding to do some shopping. He didn't actually need anything. Yes, he was running out of a few things but they could wait. But going shopping let him rationalize that he was being productive.

Work Stories

He left Sigmund in the car—He'd be embarrassed to bring a stuffed dog into Wal-Mart with its share of tough-looking customers. He got mouthwash (the store-brand version of Listerine was half the price), canned peaches in juice (The store brand too was much cheaper.)

Then, he walked the aisles for the fun of it. He considered stores to be museums where everything is for sale and cheap. You can get anything from a name-brand 65" TV for $350 to aspirin for pennies a pill. He thought, "If they gave me a million dollars, I couldn't make that."

He didn't find everything cheap and was offended when he saw something he deemed overpriced. Today, he tried on sunglasses and liked one. The price tag, hanging on a tear-proof plastic wire, was $24.95. He thought, "That's ridiculous. Those glasses must cost just pennies to make. I'd never steal from a mom-and-pop, but Wal-Mart? I can't get the pricetag off but could wear the sunglasses and tuck the pricetag under the glasses' arm so it wouldn't be very noticeable." He looked up to the ceiling, saw a store camera, and decided not to chance it.

The next morning, David didn't get to coffee until 10:50. After a quick look at the newspaper, he checked his bank account: It had dwindled to $18,000. "Sigmund, I have to work harder and market harder but can't seem to make myself. Part of it is me and part is the reality that there's a career coach under every rock. And with clients now happy to do sessions on phone and Zoom, I'm competing with the immediate universe.

"Should I go back to school? More letters next to my name would add credibility. but the years, the money, all that theory— I didn't find the undergraduate stuff that useful and this would be more esoteric." On his laptop, he looked at a respected program's curriculum: Models of Career Development, History and Systems of Personality, two graduate-level statistics courses. "I don't think so."

"Should I change careers? That's hard. My clients find it really tough unless they have an in. My only real in is with my dad, but he's a consultant to writers on word processing. Doing that work would feel like chocolate that's always an inch away— I majored in English because I like to write. Helping others to write would be frustrating. Besides, working for my dad? He'd hound me endlessly to work hard."

He looked again at A Friendly Career Guide's list of recommended career coaches. Should I ask the author if he'd include me? He doesn't know me at all, but I do know how to write. Maybe if I wrote a great letter. He does include his mailing address. He says no email, so snail mail it is: 1740 Empress Circle. Bethesda, MD 20817

> Dear Mr. Nelson (Robby?)
>
> I keep your book by my side. It's my career coaching bible. I especially like your anecdotes, the stories of everyone from dropouts to professionals to prisoners.
>
> Your writing inspired me to become a career coach. Unfortunately, to support myself, I need more clients.

You don't know me but perhaps the attached "Lessons I Learned from Robby Nelson" will convey enough expertise that you would, in your book's next edition, add me to your list of recommended career coaches.

Thank you for considering my request.

In any event, thank you for a career guide that not only is inordinately helpful but inordinately kind.

Sincerely,
David Michaels
67-05 Meadow St.
New Brunswick, NJ 08901
732-111-5724
davidcareercoach@gmail.com

David was sure that, best case, it would be at least a week until Nelson responded. So for that week, David was, as usual, indifferent to the mail's arrival. After all, it was mainly bills and junk mail: sheets of coupons for fast-food restaurants, flyers for overpriced replacement windows, and supermarket circulars hawking a couple of items at a bargain price that were often out of stock by the time you got there.

Yet on Day 6, there was a linen-finished envelope from Robert F. Nelson with his name and return address in Victorian Script font. David was surprised at the frou-frouness in light of Nelson's book's aw-shucks tone.

In addition to a letter, there was a button of the kind that supports a politician. This one bore the classic cartoon of Peanuts' Lucy with one change: "The career coach (not the psychiatrist) is in. Advice: 5 cents." And the letter from Nelson said,

> Dear David,
>
> You're right. It would be inappropriate for me to recommend you without knowing you. But I'll make you an offer. If you drive down to Bethesda to see me, stopping along the way at bars while wearing the enclosed button and have a brief career counseling session with at least three people, we can talk. You can come any day at 7:30 PM.
>
> Sincerely,
> Robert F. Nelson

"Sigmund, any day? He doesn't have a schedule? And besides, should I go? I mean, the nerve of him expecting me to drive from New Brunswick to Bethesda and stop at bars along the way to get stories. On the other hand, I guess I can understand why he might ask that as proof I'm worthy. I mean, most people of his stature probably wouldn't even have responded to my letter. Plus, I'm such a slave to my routine, it probably wouldn't hurt to break out of it for a day. It's not like I'm so busy with clients.

"Should I risk taking my car or rent a car? After all, it has 207,000 miles on it. On the other hand, it's a Toyota and my last one ran reliably for 275,000 and I only sold it because a friend was selling his Corolla with just 160,000 on it. So what if my door has a dent and the front bumper is held up by plastic ties. I'll just park it so Nelson can't see it from his window."

That night, David procrastinated and didn't set the alarm clock. His excuse was, "I have a client tomorrow." The next day, his excuse was that there was a chance of rain. But the following night, he moved the alarm clock across the room and set it for 8:00 AM.

The next morning, he was tempted to press snooze but didn't want to have to set his alarm again the next day. So he forced himself out of bed and was caffeinated and in his car by 9.

After he got past the Philly traffic, his brain had room to revisit the idea: "Sigmund, will anyone actually ask me for career help because I'm wearing a stupid 'The career coach is in' button? Will I actually help anyone? If I have to tell Nelson that I helped no one, he certainly won't include me in his book. I guess I could lie. I'm pretty scummy, aren't I?"

Soon, his eyes started to get heavy. "Sigmund, I gotta remember driver's ed: highway hypnosis. Don't stare. Keep your eyes moving— Go from left of the highway, middle, right, middle, left."

Finally, that stopped working and it was time anyway to find a bar. Where to stop? He saw the sign "Entering "Delaware." Hey, that's Biden's state. Let me see how it's doing?"

He followed the signs toward downtown and looked for a friendly-looking bar. He found The Filibuster Bar and

Grill, with a logo of a blathering politician. He parked, put on the "career coach is in" button and said, "Sigmund, you're staying in the car. It will be hard enough to be credible without a stuffed dog."

He felt like tiptoeing in but realized that wouldn't inspire confidence, so he strode. It was noon and the place was bustling with the lunch crowd. He couldn't make himself make eye contact with anyone, so he mainly stared unfocused and occasionally glanced at the staff. He noticed a woman who must have been the manager, strolling from table to table, making small talk with customers.

A few minutes later, he noticed a busser go behind the bar, grab a bottle of Wild Turkey and stick it in his backpack. "Should I tell her?"

He couldn't deal with the additional stress of having to make that decision, so he approached a prospect. He sat next to a guy at the bar who had half a bottle of cheap scotch in front of him, who downed a shot glass and then another.

"May I ask what's wrong?"

The guy looked at David's button and scoffed,

"Middle-school brass players."

"What do you mean?"

"I couldn't stand the cacophony anymore. I was so frustrated. So I took a trombone that was sitting around and fired it against the wall." A boy told the principal and she informed me that I was suspended pending termination. She explained, "If it happened again and a kid got hurt, the parent would sue."

David didn't know what to say. Silence is sometimes best and the guy continued, "So now I'm 31, two kids, stay-at-home wife, and I'm sure to get fired for throwing a trombone. I'd win Least Likely to be Hired. What's with the button?"

David explained. Then the guy said, "Okay, what should I do?"

"At least until you find a job, should your wife get a job?"

"The kids are young, she wants to be a stay-at-home-mom, and she reminds me that that was the deal."

"But you're losing your job. Could she work, (noticing a server) even as a server at least for a while until you get a job?"

He scoffed.

"I sense that you need money soon, which means no going back to school to retrain."

"Duh, Einstein."

I thought, "I won't be able to tell Nelson this story. And it's one more reminder I'm a loser. Maybe I do need to work for my father." A deep breath and David tried, "Well, the fastest route to good income without going back to school might be to look for another teaching job."

"No one will hire a teacher whose license is suspended pending investigation." He poured another.

"How about sales, maybe selling band instruments or sheet music?"

"This isn't 1950. People buy online."

I wanted to say, "Salespeople are needed for complicated products." But to avoid arguing, I restrained myself and reframed it positively: "How about selling a more complicated, big-ticket item that requires a salesperson?"

"What? I'm going to take a year to learn enterprise software? Robots?" Pointing to my button, the scotch having erased any politeness censor, he slurred, "You're not even worth five cents. Besides, I hate corporations. That's part of why I went into public school teaching."

I was getting upset with him and more insecure about myself but, in desperation, I thought hard and came up with one more try; "How about the non-profit analogue of sales: fundraising?"

"I don't like to ask people for money." He downed the glass.

"Sorry I wasn't helpful. Of course, I wish you well." And I trudged out.

Back in the car, "Sigmund, we should turn around. This won't work. On the other hand, I don't want to go back to my measly practice or even think about working for my dad. I've driven all this way— I should at least try one more bar. If I fail, I'll turn around with my tail between my legs, pardon the expression, Sigmund."

David started to get sleepy. "Sigmund, I gotta stay awake." The left-center-right cure for highway hypnosis didn't cure. He stopped for coffee, then turned the radio on, then louder, then sang along, yet still felt sleepy. Finally, he turned to a podcast, Philosophize This, and argued with the host:

"Ortega y Gasset's Mass Man is elitist, even racist!" That worked for a while but when David started to get sleepy again as he approached Baltimore. "It's time to find a bar."

He parked near the Free Spirits Saloon, stared at Sigmund and said, "Come in with me. What do I have to lose? Maybe it'll attract attention so I don't have to approach people."

He sat down wearing his button but hiding Sigmund under his jacket. But when no one came over, he pulled Sigmund out, put the button on him, and propped him up on the table.

A guy came over, noticing the iconic Lucy cartoon with the word "psychiatrist" replaced with "career coach."

He said, "I could use one."

"Tell me about it."

"I'm a cosmetic surgeon and burned out on all the politicians, climbers, and lobbyists wanting to pretty themselves up."

I didn't know what to say, so I just said, "What have you thought about doing?"

"I don't know. You're the career coach."

I thought, "I'm such a loser." That fueled my mind to race. "Maybe take a break and work for Doctors Without Borders? Do they use cosmetic surgeons?"

"No, but now that you mention it, Smile Train does— They fix kids' cleft palates in India. Thanks, guy."

I enjoyed a beer.

Back in the car and now just an hour from Nelson's home, despite being required to get three stories, he told Sigmund that he'd done enough: "If after all this driving and two good tries, Nelson doesn't want to recommend me, so be it. Who knows, maybe he'll appreciate the failure story. There's something to be learned from failure yet those rarely get published." He exhaled.

David's GPS led him to a surprise. He pictured Empress Circle being some tree-lined cul de sac of mini manses but it was Bethesda Hospital. "Sigmund, he's not an MD, so could he be a patient? He couldn't be a patient that long, could he? Sigmund, wait here." To give hospital visitors and staff a needed smile, he pushed Sigmund's legs into the steering wheel so it looked like he was driving.

As David entered the lobby, he thought, "I hate hospitals. They remind me of death, my death." At the information desk, he was told that Nelson is in the long-term care wing, room 1736.

Work Stories

David stood at 1736's closed door and wondered, "What kind of shape is Nelson in? Will he be grateful I came all the way from New York? Will that soften him enough to accept just two bar stories?

David didn't want to wait longer, which would make him conspicuous. So he forced himself to knock. A voice whispered, "In!"

Sitting in bed was an ancient man with a box of Popeye's fried chicken on his lap and a drumstick in his mouth.

"Mr. Nelson, I'm David Michaels."

"Who?"

"David Michaels." And he pulled the button from his pocket.

"Okay, where are the stories?"

David was stunned by that terseness given "Robby's" oh-so-kind book.

"Um, they're in my head."

"Write them on this laptop, one paragraph each."

Nervous, David was grateful to be given something to do, so he wrote the two paragraphs and showed them to Nelson.

"There are only two stories and in one, you failed. Thank you for coming."

David thought about arguing but decided that he wouldn't lower himself to beg this mean, hypocritical man. So he just said, "I understand."

"Fine. Thank you for the story."

"But there are two."

"I don't include failure stories. I want to give the buyers hope."

"Just curious: Have you ever asked anyone else to get anecdotes for you?"

"How do you think a 90-year-old gets all those stories for each year's edition? Did you really think I'd have a button made up just for you?"

David said, "Have a good day."

Nelson grunted.

On the drive back home, immersed in the mixed feelings of pride in how he handled Nelson and sadness about not getting into the book, David wasn't vigilant to staying at the wheel. And he nodded off, fortunately at low speed. His car bounced off a telephone pole and by the time he woke and slammed on the brakes, the car was just a foot from a boutique's picture window. Thanks to the airbag, he was okay, except that it didn't cover his arms— Both were broken. The Urgent Care's doctor set the bones and said, "You were millimeters from losing use of both arms."

It took time for that to penetrate; David was too nervous, too eager to get out of there. Urgent Care wasn't as scary as a hospital but still.

Back in his car, David took a deep breath, looked up, and said to his dead grandfather, "The broken arms are a blessing: I was close to becoming a paraplegic and that's who I'm going to specialize in: paraplegic liberal-arts majors. That is something I will work hard at. I'll also put in the work to have a real dog. I'll name it Superman after the paraplegic, Christopher Reeve. And I'll throw away everything I've shoplifted, including the Coulda Been a Contender, t-shirt. Okay, Grampa?"

A Burned-Out Teacher

Stanley Zimny, Flickr, CC2.0

It wasn't the first time that a student got up on a desk and twerked. And it wasn't even as sexual as a previous twerk. It just was the last straw. She was sick of teaching a curriculum that only suck-up kids cared about. She was sick of many students forgetting what she had painstakingly taught the day before. She was exhausted from trying to meet the needs of a huge range of students from special ed to gifted. And she was sick of the back-talk. When Rebecca was a student, an act of defiance was chewing gum in class. Now, even a twerker doesn't hesitate to sneer, "You can't make me. You ain't my mother." or "You can't touch me. I'll sue."

Rebecca had stayed in teaching only because tenure guaranteed her a salary and even a pension for life. But now, she was done. After school that day, she strode into the principal's office to quit. But he guilt-tripped her into staying for the rest of the year. And she trudged off, the weight back on her back.

But Rebecca figured she had nothing to lose, so she replaced the mandated Common Core Curriculum which is replete with pre-algebra, the history of the civil rights movement, and photosynthesis's Krebs cycle with what she called the real-life curriculum. It focused on what middle schoolers care about: friends, parents, money, and, yes, sex.

No surprise, when a fellow teacher ratted Rebecca out, the principal told her that she had to leave immediately. She asked the union to fight it but it refused, citing its contract with the school district agreeing that all teachers would teach the Common Core Curriculum in exchange for a hefty pay raise.

Rebecca became a self-employed tutor of low-income gifted kids and although she made much less money and so had to go back to living with her parents, she was happier.

Merit

My mother always told me that merit will always trump all: "Your father and I immigrated from Japan and look at us!"

Gabriel Lima, Pexels, CC0

And for a while, merit did trump all. Although I was a Japanese immigrant, I got great grades and kids liked me. Plus, I got into what they call a "highly selective" college. Quietly, I was proud of myself.

But in the required ethnic studies course and then in other courses, I was told that my pride need be restrained because I was privileged, not "earned privilege," "privileged." I was told that Black, Latinx, and Native Americans remain the victims of systemic racism and oppression. I asked one professor, "I don't feel like I'm prejudiced." She said, "You suffer from unconscious bias. After all, if you're on a dark street and you see an African-American and a Japanese-American, wouldn't you be more scared of the African-American?" I murmured yes but didn't quite see that as unfair bias, but I guess I was starting to.

After all, I did get hired as an engineer by a quality company. They paid me well, good benefits, provided training. Very few Blacks, Latinx, and Native Americans did. And so much in the news and entertainment media portrays BIPOCs as victims who triumph only because of superior ability or spunk. Could they be all wrong and my parents and I be right?

And when we took the required diversity, equity, and inclusion training, I was feeling so guilty that I cried in the session. The leader then asked me if I'd like to be on a hiring committee.

I felt taken up by the cause of social "justice" and believed that increasing not just equality but equity required giving preference to BIPOC candidates. So whenever I could, I voted for and later championed BIPOC candidates even when it was a job I wanted.

I didn't really stop to think about the more qualified candidates who got rejected, the coworkers who would be saddled with less able or hard-working employees, or the customers who got a worse product or service. I somehow just thought of it as reparations.

But overall, I feel good about giving up some of my privilege. And I look forward to when oppressed people get cash reparations from the taxpayer.

I had long been afraid to tell my mother about my evolved views but one day after work, I did. She simply said, "You're wrong. America is wrong. Now let's have dinner."

All-Star

I made the all-star team seven years ago but now I'm old, don't got my same game: I ain't gettin' open for my jumper, I ain't stutter-steppin' to the can so fast and, on d, I get beat more.

Kick Photo, Flickr, CC2.0

But I'm scared of retirin'. I see what happens: The endorsements go away, you get fat, and you buy a car dealership— And all they want is your name. You're useless— big come-down.

So I hung on— I went from all-star to 11th man— I only got in when the game was over and coach didn't want to risk a good player getting hurt.

But coach decided for me: He put me on waivers and no one claimed me.

I ain't no sit-around guy so, same day, I asked my agent about playing EuroLeague. He said they'd pay me shit and that I should open a car dealership. Fuck him. Unless I make him big money, I'm just garbage. He ate the orange and now he's throwing away the peel? Fuck him!

I asked my college coach if he wanted me as an assistant coach. He said he was glad I called and he'd get back to me. Bullshit— He never got back to me. My high school coach said, "Anthony, you were born with springs in your legs, not in your mouth."

Should I go back to college? I hated college—They only let me in because I could hoop—After one year, I got out of there—entered the draft—1st round pick, man.

Should I just retire and live off my money? Naw, I spend too much. I'll be broke. I know me—I ain't gonna control myself and do me cheap.

Now that I'm not playing, I'm already eatin' too much-Like yesterday, I ate a whole large Domino's. I can see how we become tubs of lard.

I think I'll call some other NBA retired guys and see what they say.

A Dropout

I dropped out of college. It wasn't just the money, although that was crazy-high. It was mainly that I didn't care about academics.

Courtesy, Wade Photography

But I do I like reading. So while trying to figure out what who I am and what I wanted to do, I walked into my local library and asked if they'd give me a job. They did. My main job had nothing to do with books. If one of the homeless people was there for too long and smelled of piss or B.O., my job was to ask the person to leave and offer a sheet of resources for the homeless.

The best part of my job was putting books back on the shelves. All those books were up-close and I could borrow them for free!

I decided to focus on basketball coaching. I started with one skinny book meant for high school kids, but that made me comfortable. Then, at the library's computer, articles and videos on coaching.

Next, I went back to my high school basketball coach and asked if I could volunteer. She said I could do stuff like collect the towels and other laundry — You gotta start somewhere.

I also asked the coach questions about coaching. I guess she liked that because soon, she let me sit on the bench. I asked more questions and cheered my team a lot. And I watched more videos on coaching.

Then, I decided to go back to school to study coaching. On the internet, I found a few colleges that had a major in coaching and I applied. As I am writing to you, I'm a student at a place I'd never would have imagined: Miami University of Ohio. Its nickname: "The Cradle of Coaches."

A Cheery Chemo Nurse

In the hospital's changing room, Denise replaced her no-nonsense gray sweats with the pink and purple nurse's uniform she chose for this job.

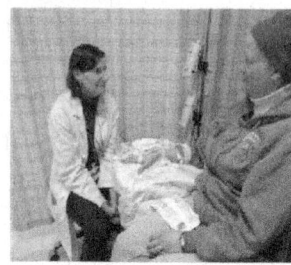

Kbrookes, Flickr, CC2.0

She padded into the empty chemotherapy room and turned on music that was pleasant but not so chipper that its intent to distract was too obvious.

Then Denise plastered on the smile she had perfected by practicing in a mirror and stepped into the waiting room for chemo patients.

"Janet Rodgers?" A 32-year-old who doesn't look like she has cancer peered up at Denise. Janet's fear flashed and, embarrassed, she made herself mirror Denise's fake smile and followed her into the chemo room.

As Denise was hooking her up, Janet asked, "The doctor told me I won't vomit much but it couldn't hurt to have a second opinion." Denise consulted her chart and said, "Doc's right. No biggie."

Then Janet asked, "One more question: I just had a baby. My doctor said I can't breastfeed while doing chemo. Right? I was looking forward to breastfeeding." Denise nodded: Breast milk won't transmit cancer but the chemo wouldn't be so good for the baby. Janet, you're Stage 1, you're getting mild chemo, you'll be fine!"

Denise returned to the waiting room. "Michael Sanders?" A swarthy 55-year-old strode in, face-neutral.

To break the ice and distract him while she was setting up, Denise asked, "So Mr. Sanders, anything you want to tell me about yourself?"

"I had big dreams to create a heated sweater so instead of having to heat the entire house or office, you only heat what counts: you. I had that dream until this."

Denise replied, "Lots of people with Stage 2 do just fine. I hope you won't give up your dream." He was silent as she inserted the needle.

"Harold Goldman?" A man who looked 80 lifted his hand. Denise helped him up and into the room. She looked at his chart: He was only 68 but had had two cancer surgeries, two rounds of radiation, and this was to be his third round of chemo— an experimental, side-effect-heavy protocol that's approved only for end-stage patients. Denise reverted to a standard introduction, "Mr. Goldman, how are you feeling today?" He said, "How do you think?" whereupon she said, sounding more chipper than she intended, "Okay, let's do this?" He said, "Okay, you first." She appreciated the humor but stopped smiling when he mumbled, "I, I, I can't do this anymore." And he struggled to his feet. "Mr. Goldman, please sit down." And he limped out.

Twenty-one more patients and Denise changed back into her sweats. In the peace of her car, she flashed on her husband who died a year ago in pain, of cancer, despite or perhaps exacerbated by the side effects of the poison she puts into people's arms every day. She thought, "Please God, don't let me get cancer," and she put on her mix-tape of pep-me-up music, starting with "Celebrate!"

A Psychiatrist's Last Hour

The patient sobbed, "Thank you for understanding how tough it's been for me since she died."

I thought, "It's been a year, and it's a rabbit."

With permission, 18/1 Graphics Studio

"Every time I think about moving forward, I think of Carrots and I cry."

"I understand. Unfortunately, we're out of time for today. Is there anything you want to remember from today's session?"

"I don't know. Dr. Michaels, is it normal to grieve so long?

I would have liked to ask, "Might that be an excuse to keep from looking for a job?" but I felt he'd just get defensive, so I just said, "We all process differently. For homework, is there anything you'd like to try?"

"I should try to get a job, and this time I will." I doubted it.

"Uh, can you refill my prescription?"

"It's time to cut down to 10 milligrams."

"I really need 20. I'm so stressed. Dr. Michaels, please!"

I was too tired to fight: "All right, the last prescription at 20."

"Oh thank you, thank you, Dr. Michaels."

"See you next week."

The client strode out.

I bowed my head.

When I got home, I stared at my front door. Why so ornate? Who am I trying to impress?

On opening the door, I got my usual warm welcome from my doggie Tarzan, who leaped not through trees but onto me.

When I dropped into my recliner, Tarzan on my lap, I thought, "Why do I do all this: killed myself in school, in college, in med school and residency, and work really hard now? I don't feel I'm making much difference. Why have I done it all? So I can live in a nice place? What does it all mean? Does anything mean anything? Oh, I have to appeal those denials of coverage. Excuse me, Tarzan."

I shuffled to my desk, he followed and rested his head on my foot.

While writing to Aetna, Tarzan vomited a grass-filled blob. I sighed, "Dog parenthood."

I blotted, rinsed, repeated, sprayed, washed hands, and returned to begging Aetna.

But Tarzan vomited again the next day, so it was off to the vet. The vet said, "It's probably nothing."

"No need for tests?"

"It's not worth the discomfort and expense of an endoscopy. You're a doc, you know: Most times it's a horse, not a zebra."

But the next two days, Tarzan kept vomiting and without the reassuring grass.

The vet said, "I still think it's nothing but let's do the endoscopy."

"All normal. I'm sure Tarzan will be fine."

But two more days of vomiting and I made an appointment with a specialist vet. The first opening was two weeks out.

***

"David, there is a lesion here. Somehow, the other vet missed it. We should do a whole-body scan." "Stage 4."

"Thank you, Doctor. At least now I know."

Back home, I cradled Tarzan." I won't sue the first vet- I've made mistakes too." Fighting my shaking hand, I opened my book-safe, pulled out the fentanyl vial, and helped my best friend avoid end-stage cancer's pain.

I filled the syringe again, this time completely, put it aside, and wrote:

Dear fellow psychiatrists,

I worried my way through life, stressed my way through life, to try to become a decent psychiatrist. I traded most pleasure for accomplishment.

I do not think it was worth it.

It may be that I wasn't a good-enough psychiatrist but it seems that many of us don't accomplish enough for all our time, brains, and effort. Too often, our drugs and "procedures" are mere palliatives.

It's no shame to leave psychiatry— Don't throw more good time and effort after bad. Even being a good cafe owner will likely bring more pleasure to your customers and employees. Just use your good brain and drive, and be kind.

David Michaels

"Now I'll put myself at peace."

***

When David didn't show up at work nor answer his page, his boss, the hospital's chief of psychiatry, called the police, which found David and the note. The officer sent it to David's boss, who posted it on websites for aspiring psychiatrists.

Boring Man

Public Domain Pictures, CC0

Sal is a package reboxer for Luxe d' Italia, which sells high-end leather, jewelry, and stemware. When customers return items, Sal's job is to inspect them to see if they're in salable condition and then rebox them so they look like new.

Sal is in his 22nd year on that job and likes the stability and security. The company is ever growing, continually improving its search-engine optimization and shopping interface, as well as its Google and Facebook ads.

Sal's main recreation is bocce. He goes twice a week to the Italian-American Social Club's bocce court, where he plays two games. The conversation is limited mainly to the likes of, "Good roll," "What's the score?" and "See you next time."

Then, two things happened within a month of each other that disrupted Sal's stasis. A consultant said that it's more efficient for each reboxer to have fewer types of packages to rebox. Sal was already bored with his job but that pushed him to find *some* sort of novelty. And then, his wife left him because she was, well, bored with Sal.

Sal had never done much on social media let alone on the cool Instagram or TikTok. Because he didn't know how to make videos, he chose Instagram, which allows text messages.

He described himself as a 16-year-old girl, "Sally," joined a group of similar girls, read their posts, and then started to post and to respond. He started with safe messages, for example, "What's your favorite outfit?" and a girl named Tina wrote, "OMG. Crop Tops!!!!!!!"

But then he decided to be more substantive, asking about parents, friends, drugs, sex. One girl, Mia, responded ever more often. And then she wrote, "I'm so glad you ask about this stuff. It's what I think about and your answers are, like, so mature."

Sal, feeling flattered, scared, and responsible, decided he'd better tell her who he is, even though that would probably mean that she'd ghost him forever. Her response: "You're the friend I wish I had, the dad I wish I had."

Sal wrote back, "I'm flattered. Feel free to message me but you'll need to take the lead. I certainly don't want to be a stalker."

They exchanged a few more direct messages, each a little lighter, and finally, they agreed to stop.

Sal decided he wanted more modest changes. So he told his boss that he needed to be given the full range of boxes to rebox or he'd quit, and the boss agreed. Sal quit the bocce group and joined a softball team. And he went on match.com to look for a nice woman even if, perhaps especially if, she's a little boring.

A Lonely College President

I never aspired to be president, college or otherwise. but the timing was good: They were looking for a woman and a liberal but not someone so Leftist that alumni would stop giving.

Ted Eytan, CC 4.0

People don't realize that it's lonely being president. People are intimidated to interact with me, or they suck up, or they attack me because they want my job or because of politics.

For example, after a frustrating week, I asked a VP who I thought I could trust out for a drink. After my second glass of wine, I said that I'm thinking that Wokeness is going too far, like on the trans athlete issue.

Well, at the next Faculty Senate meeting, someone quoted that and denounced me: "Our leader isn't anti-racist?! Isn't a trans advocate! That is unaligned with our focus on diversity, equity, and inclusion! It's not aligned with the pledge we require every applicant to make! We must issue a vote of no-confidence!" And they did, and "encouraged" me to resign the presidency—"If you go back to the classroom, we'll leave it at that."

I'm not a fighter, so I did go back to teaching. I teach writing, but from an only moderately liberal perspective.

Work Stories

My classes have a few older students and one of them, a thoughtful man named Jeremy, came up to me after class and asked if I'd like to go out for coffee with him.

I'll be going on my fourth date with Jeremy and can say that for now at least, this former college president isn't feeling lonely.

Redistributor

I teach high school history and, after school, coach the track team.

I've long been onboard with liberal thinking, so I support the new curriculum.

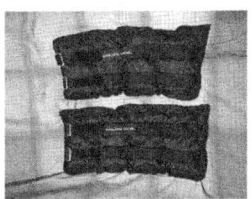

Ankle weights, Chen Zhao, Wikimedia, CC 2.0

In class, I emphasize white men's oppression of people of color. I make a point of calling on BIPOCs (Black and indigenous people of color) and, because they still are the victims of the legacy of slavery and today's systemic racism, I give them better grades. For example, if a white would get an F, I give a BIPOC a D.

On my track team, to help whites feel the oppression that BIPOCs are victims of, I have the white runners wear ankle weights. And because privilege can extend beyond race to class, I also have the fast runners of whatever race wear ankle weights. We need to fight not for equality but for equity.

I am proud that I am part of the large and growing collective effort to make next generation more egalitarian, without judgment, of all people, especially BIPOCs.

And yet...

We just had a ten-year reunion of my students. I asked, "So, looking back, what do you think of my classes or my track coaching?" Overwhelmingly, the BIPOCs said that I was the best teacher they ever had. Most of the white and Asian students said I was the worst: anti-merit, unfair., making them feel unfairly guilty, sacrificing, and the world worse. Some said they're still angry with me now, ten years later.

While I Can

My neighbor is an old guy, like maybe 70. He mainly sits around but every so often, I see him trudge to his car with a duffel bag.

RawPixel, CC0

I'm kind of scared of old people, so I ignore him. Actually, I try to avoid him, and if I can't, I just say hi, he nods, and I keep walking.

But once, he dropped his duffel as he was trying to load it into his car. I saw him strain in bending down, so I asked him if he needed help. He said, "Thank you." So I put the duffel in his car and started to walk away but he stopped me. He said, "Son, I see you a lot during the day. Why aren't you working or in school?"

The truth is that I'm shit at school—They call it dyslexia but I know it's not just that. Anyway, the last thing I want to do is go to college—High school was hard enough.

I know I should get a job, any job—in a warehouse, delivery driver, coffee shop, whatever—but even though my parents are giving me hell, I can't make myself look hard. I sometimes get a job interview, but they can tell I'm not really into it. Of course, I didn't tell the old man that. I just said, "I'm figuring out what I want to do."

But that got him going: "I'm a piano tuner and am beginning to lose it—My hands are shaking a little and worse, so's my mind. I've been looking for an apprentice to pass on what I know—while I can—but no young person is interested in learning how to tune pianos— Pianos are as they say, "Old school." One young woman who turned me down asked, 'But can you teach me how to repair synthesizer workstations?' Hah. Might you like to at least see what I do?"

He was right, I couldn't care less about pianos. My only musical instrument is my iPhone. But I was bored and didn't want to say no to the guy, so I said okay.

Tuning is so detailed. I mean, each key has two or three strings and each one has to be tuned separately. You have to move the pin that holds each string very slightly left or right. Then you have to tighten each pin a little more and then loosen it a bit so the strings will stay in tune. The truth is, even if the piano was cool like it was 200 years ago, tuning is too detail-oriented for me.

But after he tuned the piano, he asked me if I wanted to be his apprentice. Because I had nothing better to do, didn't want to say no to the old man, and especially because it would get my parents off my back, I said okay.

It's 40 years later, he died a long time ago, and I'm still a piano tuner. Now, I'm looking for an apprentice. Know anyone?

The 50-Year Secretary, Oops, Admin

I think the administration assigned Helen to me because both of us are in a wheelchair, but we ended up compatible in more important ways.

GetArchive, Public Domain

Her strengths compensate for my weaknesses. While I'm good at coming up with ideas, I can be disorganized, while she's a bit of a neat freak. I am enthusiastic but that occasionally devolves into anger, while Helen is steady. I'm serious to a fault—She's moderate.

Glaciers move faster than universities. The two of us have seen many trivial changes that the university considers major but that we laugh at:

For example, when we started, we were Southwest Kansas College. Then, although nothing much had changed, they changed the name to Southwest Kansas State University—I guess it sounded better to prospective students and donors. And recently, they changed it to John F. Kennedy State University. Now that the university has a marketing department, I'm guessing they found that JFK State U polls better.

Then there was the time that the administration sent all faculty and staff a memo ordering all faculty to "henceforth refer to the people who previously were termed secretaries as 'administrative assistants.'" Helen's reaction: "Don't administrators have anything better to do with their time and students' and taxpayers' money than that?!" I love Helen.

Then there was the time when they paraded us "differently abled workers" into a Diversity, Equity, and Inclusion (DEI) meeting—We felt like zoo animals. We couldn't wait to escape—and we left work early and went out for a drink.

Helen had been my secretary, oops, admin, for 49 years and we had agreed that we'd retire together when we hit 50. Unfortunately, administration didn't care about that. Seven months before that, I received a notice that because my external grants had declined, the university would no longer support both Helen and me.

I offered to be the one who retired, but Helen refused. She offered to retire and I refused. We decided that the number 50 was meaningless and, happily, we rolled out together.

"Should I Follow My Dad or Mom?"

I had always thought I'd follow my dad and become a doctor. But then, my mother divorced my dad because, "You're never home, and when you are, half the time, your damn pager goes off."

RawPixel, CC0

So there I was, staring at the Common Application, the form that lets you apply to lots of colleges with one application. And there was the question: intended major. Before the divorce, I was sure I'd pick pre-med. But now? My mother gives piano lessons and she seems happier than he is. But is happiness all that counts? I mean saving lives is more important than flogging kids to learn sonatinas.

But the status thing and, okay, the money thing, made me pick pre-med. And even when the pre-med courses were much harder than I imagined the music courses would have been, I stayed with it.

Then I met Judy. I'll spare you the details but we fell in love. Her major was landscape architecture, which sounded like an easier major and a better if less prestigious career than doctor: lower stress, outdoors a lot, no pager calls. And piano teacher or musician? Too much of a cliche, too low paying. Besides, it felt romantic to major in what my girlfriend was majoring in.

Now, it's a decade later and Judy and I have long broken up but I am a landscape architect. I guess it's true that many people don't choose a career. It just happens.

A School Bus Driver

Hippopx, CC0

Even when the kids weren't yelling or fighting, the accretive effect of 30 kids, 30 minutes each way, five days a week, 177 days a year, for seven years now, is wearing. A clear sign was when Devon wondered, "Would the world be better or worse if I drove the bus off the cliff?"

One day, when the bus arrived at school, a slight boy, Jeremy, said to Devon, "You always look sad, even mad."

Devon's first reaction was embarrassment but then was impressed with Jeremy's other-directedness. Most kids, indeed most adults, care only about themselves or just temporarily for someone they want to befriend.

Devon didn't want to reveal his dark thoughts about bus driving yet wanted to be somewhat revealing, so he said, "I'd always hoped I could be a limo driver, getting to meet famous people or just seeing couples going to the prom. I also wanted to have kids but the right situation never came up. So you guys are my kids, even though the noise does frustrate me."

Jeremy then revealed something about himself: He explained that he was a loner, uncomfortable with and, even at a young age, cynical about kids' motives, so he became bookish, an acceptable way to not be social.

For fear of starting too much of a relationship with a student, Devon thanked Jeremy and decided that he would try to have good conversations with other kids.

The Biggest Molecule

My father died, too young, of cancer, and that motivated me to spend my life trying to prevent the dreaded disease.

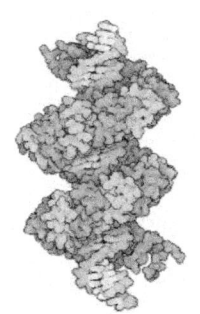

David Goodsell, Wikimedia, CC 3.0

And I failed. Avenue after avenue—from gene to circuit to environmental influences—All that my 850 experiments accomplished was to close 850 blind alleys.

But finally, I tried this long-term experiment. I identified 100 healthy people 70 to 80, old enough that a number of them would likely get some cancer in the next decade. I took a cell sample from each person and analyzed them thoroughly—even the so-called junk DNA that sits between the clearly functional parts. Every year for the next ten, I collected a new cell sample from each person and analyzed them the same way.

After ten years, 17 of the 100 were diagnosed with a cancer. I compared the annual changes in those people's cells with the changes in cells of people who did not have cancer. It turned out that in 86 percent of the cancer patients, a molecule in the junk DNA that was previously thought non-functional, changed far more over the decade. Further analysis explained what was going on: Those changes in that part of the DNA destroyed the inhibitor that prevents normal cells from duplicating too rapidly—what we call cancer. Amazingly, that occurred across a wide range of cancers.

Identifying that molecular reaction made it relatively easy to create a drug that would prevent those changes. And because I identified that foundational mechanism, the drug would have no side effects—It would act only on that molecule in the junk DNA. In simple terms, I found a vaccine to prevent cancer.

Alas, that is merely my vision. It's the essay on my application to become a student in a Ph.D. program in molecular genetics. May it turn out to be true.

Made in the USA
Coppell, TX
29 March 2024